A Christmas Gift

A Yuletide Creek Series

Kimberly Thomas

Chapter One

Nicole sputtered the lukewarm coffee she was drinking, almost spilling the liquid onto her scrubs. "Darn it!" she hissed as she managed to maneuver herself fast enough.

She'd just remembered the X-ray images she'd sent for printing. She quickly set the cup on the counter and dashed to the printer. The lab door crashed against the wall as she charged breathlessly to the copy room.

"He almost beat you to it," Sarah, the technician, giggled as she breezed past her down the hall.

"Not funny, Sarah," Nicole replied as she slid to the door and rushed inside. They were still there. She sighed with relief, swiftly picked them up, and then left the room.

She was just in time. Dr. Anthony walked hurriedly out of his office, his head buried in the file he held in his hand, and headed straight for her. He looked up just as he got to her, as if he had been expecting her to be there waiting for him. He smirked and held out his hand.

"You actually got it this time," he said.

She clenched her jaw, forced a smile, and slapped the images into his hand.

He didn't say thanks. He never did. He simply buried his head in the folder once more and walked off.

"You're welcome," she called out after him.

He grunted, then turned the corner. Nicole turned back around and headed for the small office in the lab she shared with Sarah.

"Such a douche!" Sarah complained.

Nicole sat on the swivel stool, feeling annoyed. She picked up the coffee cup and gazed inside, but it was ruined. She dumped the contents and sat back down to look over the other clients that she had scheduled for the day.

"Why do you let him talk to you like that?" Sarah finally turned and asked, probably out of frustration. "You're one of the best technicians here at the clinic. You're always on time. You never give crappy images. You're never ever rude, although I don't understand why..."

"Ugh," Nicole grunted and rubbed her forehead. "I don't want to get into it now, Sarah," she moped. "I'm tired. It's been a long day, and I just want to go home, soak myself in the hot tub, and pretend none of this exists."

"He should treat you better. That's all I'm saying," Sarah persisted as she pouted her pink lips.

Nicole glanced sideways at her. Sarah's head was lowered, and her golden ponytail brushed against her shoulders. "Thanks," she finally said.

"Pssh!" Sarah hissed, waving her off. "You're too nice," she said, widening her eyes at her. "*That's* your problem."

"Yeah, that or I'm just an idiot." Nicole sighed. "Excuse me. I have another patient."

"I have a few scans to run myself," Sarah replied as she got up.

Nicole sighed to herself as she walked out of the office and into the lobby. Sarah wasn't wrong. Dr. Anthony wasn't the best person to work with. She was good at her job, but she never really felt appreciated. Lucky for her, she wasn't doing it for him.

But she still didn't understand why she put up with his arrogance and rudeness. It wasn't as if she couldn't get a job somewhere else.

But she enjoyed helping her patients in any way she could, even if it meant she had to work for Dr. Grouch. She felt hopeful when she saw the next name on the schedule. It was one of her favorite clients.

"Lilian Weber?" Nicole called when she got to the waiting room.

"Here," a silver-haired woman said as she struggled to a stand. The gentleman next to her jumped up and assisted her in grabbing her cane.

"Thanks, dear." She smiled, patting his hand as she wobbled over to a smiling Nicole.

"Hello, Lily," Nicole beamed at the woman.

Her eyes twinkled with pleasure when she saw Nicole. "Oh, if it isn't the nice one," she said as her freckled, wrinkly face lit up. "How are you?"

"I'm doing great," Nicole replied. "But as usual, we're doing this in reverse." The woman cackled as Nicole pushed open the double doors. "Okay, so we're here to check that hip of yours. How are you feeling?"

"Oh, you know." She hobbled over to the station. "I've had better days."

"I'm sure you have," Nicole said. "You know the drill. I'll give you some privacy to get undressed.

"Okay, thank you," she replied. "I hope this is the last time. I've been feeling better."

"That's great, Lily," Nicole told the woman.

"Don't I know it. I don't want to be stuck hobbling around during Christmas when my grandbabies are here."

"Oh, right, Christmas," Nicole returned absent-mindedly.

Lilian whipped her head around. "Don't tell me you forgot about Christmas. It's only a month away," she said with disappointment.

"No, I didn't," Nicole lied. "I just didn't realize how quickly the time was passing."

But she did forget. That year and the past ten before that. She'd forgotten about Christmas since her parents got a divorce— because of her.

She clenched her jaw and forced the awful memories back where they belonged— in the darkest recesses of her mind.

"All right, let's get you up on that table, shall we?"

She'd allowed Lilian some privacy to get undressed before helping her onto the examination table. Her thoughts drifted as she waited for the machine to take a scan of Lilian's body.

She used to love Christmas. A very long time ago. Back when she was a child in Yuletide Creek. She'd lived a very idyllic childhood, where everything seemed to be made out of rainbows and cotton candy. Her parents had given her every child's dream. She had more than she needed and felt she held their constant attention. They doted on her all of the time, and come Christmastime, they never held back. She got more presents than the average child, even though she didn't have siblings to play with.

She remembered how her mother would bake cookies, gingerbread houses, and mince pies. She'd help her to make cranberry molds and dress the turkey. And that had been her life for years. It was as if she lived in a bubble.

A bubble that burst when she introduced the pin.

She sighed when she remembered staring into the oak tree, her heart in her mouth, and the hood of the car twisted out of shape and smoking. Someone had come and dragged her out of the ruins— she could barely feel herself move. She'd lost all her senses. And after that, everything went downhill in her family. She'd overheard the arguments surrounding it— how her mother had stood up for her and how her father thought she wasn't being hard enough on Nicole.

But it wasn't just in her family. The traditions in the small town had waned over time as more people left, but some still remained, like the annual Christmas House that went on display, the gingerbread house, and the like. She wasn't even sure if they still did those things. She hadn't been back since she was nineteen.

How could I? After what I'd done?

Christmas had become just another day for her, and even more so since her own marriage fell apart and her daughter, Stevie, moved away to college. It was as if there was nothing to be gay and jolly about anymore, and it was hard for her to feign cheerfulness when all Christmas did was bring bitter memories of her family falling apart.

And her boss didn't help her dismal outlook at all! In fact, he was a gross contributor.

"Are we done?" Lilian's voice broke through the din in her mind.

"Oh, yes, sorry," she snapped out of her reverie. She helped Lilian off the table, and in minutes, the woman was ready to go. "All right, we'll have those images sent to Dr. Anthony, and he'll reach out to you as soon as possible."

"Okay, dear," Lilian replied, reaching for her cane. "I hope you cheer up." She smiled. "You're too pretty not to smile."

Nicole's heart warmed by the old woman's compliment. "Thanks, Lilian. Have a great day. I'll walk you out."

She followed her out, but the fact that she'd brought up Christmas only opened a can of worms for Nicole. After her parents' divorce, she'd left Yuletide Creek and had fallen head over heels for Rudy, the bad-boy-turned-grunge-musician. She couldn't bear to be there anymore when she was the one who caused them to get divorced in the first place.

If she hadn't sneaked out with the car— if she hadn't been such a pain— if she'd been a better daughter, then they'd still be married, and she couldn't watch her mother crying every day. The guilt had become too much, so it was no wonder she sought escape with a traveling band. Rudy had been stunning, with his dark hair and smoky eyes, driving her insane every time he looked her way. Even worse when he played songs that he'd written specifically for her.

She decided then she'd marry him, and he agreed. Her mother didn't, and they'd fought about that too. Her mother didn't like Rudy— didn't think he would make her happy. Guilt and shame ripped her apart. Despite her mother's disapproval, she was happy with Rudy, and she didn't want to rub that in her mother's face when she'd been the source of her unhappiness of late.

They had a whirlwind affair up until when Stevie was born two years later.

She hadn't known what she was doing, and having a baby didn't help. Rudy had to be on the road all the time, which left her home a lot with Stevie. She couldn't be there for his shows like before, and pretty soon, he started hooking up with his groupies.

It was a mistake at first. *"Something that just happened,"* he'd told her. *"It won't happen again. I promise."*

But it did.

Then, when he was drunk, his favorite line was: *Please forgive me.*

And she did.

I was lonely.

That was when she lost it. He wasn't going to stop. She couldn't satisfy him anymore. He needed more, and she had a daughter to raise. She couldn't be to him what he wanted— which was all fun, games, and parties.

She held it together for as long as she could. But every marriage took two for it to work, and Rudy was never there. He started going home less and less until, just before Christmas, five years ago, he'd told her he wasn't coming back.

And that was it. She was left with the task of explaining to their daughter why he'd walked out and why he wasn't coming back. She had to make Christmas fun for Stevie over the years that followed, but when Stevie left, Christmas was the last thing she wanted to celebrate.

She was glad when the day came to an end. She

quickly packed up and left the office before Dr. Anthony found her and forced her to stay after hours digging up files or reprinting images. She swore he was put in her life to torment her.

She slipped into her coat just before she walked outside the building. It was nippy, as it was prone to be in Seattle at that time of year. She wrapped her scarf tighter around her neck and slipped her hands into her coat pocket as she dashed around the building to the parking lot.

The temperature was forty-five degrees, but it felt like forty. She dreaded the winter— had always hated it. She figured winter, the snow, and the ice were for people who enjoyed the season. All she had was the cold.

She got to her black Nissan Rogue and hopped inside, grateful for the remote control that had the car heated before she got in.

She rubbed her palms together, waiting a few seconds to shake the cold that had clung to her in her one-minute walk from the office.

The traffic was smooth on her eight-minute drive home, which was weird for a Monday evening, but she was appreciative when she saw her townhouse come into view. She'd thought about getting something smaller but decided against it. Stevie might return home after college.

But for the moment, she had a hot date with the bathtub, a glass of wine, and some candles.

She kicked off her shoes as soon as she walked in, hung her coat and purse in the closet behind the door, and headed straight for her master bedroom, which had its own bath.

She slipped out of her scrubs, pinned her auburn hair at the top of her head, and wrapped herself in her downy bathrobe. Her bed slippers were next to the closet door, and she stepped into them and headed for the kitchen for her faithful companions.

"Dom, it's me and you again tonight," she whispered to the bottle of Dom Perignon wine right before she opened the cupboard and found its matching piece.

The clock read six thirty, and some may have thought it too early for wine. But she had all night and more bottles— time was no longer a factor.

She ran the bath, added her scented oils, and was about to step inside when she caught a glimpse of herself in the mirror.

Sorrowful brown eyes stared back at her. Her oval face was more pronounced with her hair pinned at the top of her head, and she turned her face from side to side, checking out the pale freckles that were around her nose. She didn't think she was a bad-looking woman. Her five-foot, six inches height was perfectly supported by her one hundred and sixty pounds. She was okay with that number for the most part, but she was wondering if anyone else was.

She hadn't had a date since Rudy walked out, and the divorce papers followed. She sighed— maybe she was losing her attractiveness to the opposite sex. Not that she was sure she'd want to date either. She'd given her best years to Rudy. All she had left were memories, and a great deal of them were depressing.

Nicole stepped into the bath and slid into the foamy water. She'd just poured her first glass of wine and was about to take a sip when she heard her phone ring.

"Oh, come on!" she shouted at the room. She hated how the phone never rang until she had settled into a comfortable position somewhere. And it was never close to her.

The phone was on her bed, and it kept ringing. She couldn't ignore it. It wasn't her style. She closed her eyes tightly and tried to force her nature into submission— maybe they'd leave a message. They'd quit after the second time. But her curiosity got the better of her, especially since the caller didn't quit.

She groaned and got out of the tub, her body dripping wet, and padded into the bedroom. She sucked in a deep breath when she saw who the caller was— her mother.

They hadn't spoken in weeks. Nicole sighed and stared at the device for a few seconds before she worked up the nerve to answer. "Hi, Mom," she answered softly.

"Nicole. Hi, sweetie," Trisha replied. And then there was silence.

Nicole never knew what to say to her. And for years, it had been like that. Her shame and guilt over the divorce had kept her away. And it wasn't just that. Her mother had been right about Rudy, too, to compound the shame.

"How are you?" she asked as she stood in the center of the room, naked. It was the only neutral thing she could think to ask.

"Honey, why don't you come home?" Trisha asked.

Nicole sighed. "You know why, Mom. Let's not do this now."

"You always say it's because you're busy. You can't be that busy," Trisha sulked on the other end of the phone. It tore Nicole to pieces.

The door to her returning home had been open all along, but the guilt wouldn't allow her to walk through it, so she'd used the only excuse she could find— she was busy, and her schedule wouldn't allow it. But she knew the excuse was lame, even to her mother, and she could feel that it wasn't going to cut it that time.

"Mom, I don't know," Nicole replied, then pinched the bridge of her nose. "I have work, and I can't just up and leave. I have patients."

"You're not the doctor," Trisha insisted. "Don't you have personal time off? Take a few days. You and Stevie, come spend Christmas with me this year."

That invitation didn't help sway Nicole. Christmas with her mom would only make her feel worse. "I don't know. I'll think about it."

Trisha sighed. "I miss my girls. And I barely see Stevie. What is she now, twenty-one?"

"Twenty-two," Nicole corrected her.

"I bet she gets Christmas off. How about it? It's just me, and it's just you two when it can be us three girls. It'll be fun."

Nicole didn't equate fun with Christmas— just the blues. But she heard the desperation in her mother's voice. She knew what it was like to be alone. Maybe she should really think about visiting for Christmas. Maybe just the weekend.

"I also need help with the shop, but that's not the main reason," Trisha was quick to right herself.

"The shop? What's wrong with the shop?" She knew her mother had opened up an antique shop after she'd left, which Nicole never understood. She hadn't known her mother to be a businesswoman, so she wasn't surprised at all that she needed help.

"Nothing's wrong with the shop, really," Trisha replied tentatively. "It's just that there are so many things, and I'm losing track of stuff."

"Mom," Nicole wailed. "I thought we talked about this. You don't even need that shop in the first place."

"I did," she insisted. "You wouldn't understand."

Nicole exhaled and stared at the forgotten glass of wine that was sweating and slowly becoming warm. "I know you wanted to stay busy, but you could have done gardening. I'd even have understood you running a bakery or helping out in one. I told you running a shop wouldn't be easy."

"But I already had a lot of stuff that I collected over the years, so an antique shop made sense. And there weren't any other ones in town. It would just mean a lot to me if you could come and help me out."

"I know what you're doing, Mom," Nicole told her. "You just want to get me there for Christmas. You could have asked me at any other time."

Trisha chuckled. "Guilty, but can you blame me? This way, you can kill two birds with one stone."

Nicole sighed. "Mom, it doesn't even make sense to keep the shop. Do you even get sales? It's a small town. How many antique things can you sell to the same people?"

"I'd sell more if I could keep track of things," Trisha persisted. "Or if I had help."

Nicole was finding it harder to keep refusing her the longer she kept asking. Her mother had never asked much of her since she'd left, so maybe she could consider it. Also, with all that was going on at the clinic, maybe it would be good to just get away and take a break.

"Okay, how about I come visit for Christmas? While I'm there, I can give you an assessment of the shop, and if necessary, you can consider possibly selling the place?" Nicole finally asked.

"You're actually coming?" Trisha asked excitedly. "Oh, goodie!" Nicole could hear her mother clapping through the phone, then her laughter of joy.

Nicole was locked in. She couldn't back out again. Plus, it was good to hear the happiness in her mother's voice. If anything, maybe she owed her for all the hurt she'd caused her. She really did miss her.

"Yes, Mom," she drawled. "I'll call Stevie, and we'll come."

"This is going to be so wonderful to have you both here. It's going to be the most marvelous Christmas in such a long time, sweetie," Trisha gushed.

Nicole could already see her announcing it to the neighbors and anyone that would listen, and she smiled to herself.

Visiting Yuletide Creek may not be such a bad thing.
Even if it was for the last time!

Chapter Two

When Nicole stepped outside the airport, there was an instant wave of nostalgia that hit her. The last time she was there, she was leaving.

With Rudy.

Now she was returning alone. Her heart sank as the memories flooded her mind— all the ones of how their love had blossomed quickly, like a flower that only bloomed once in their life every ten years, then faded like the morning mist.

But she wouldn't think about that. It was almost Christmas, not time to dwell on the past.

"Taxi?" a yellow cab driver waved and called to her as she pulled her suitcase after her.

"No, thanks," she replied and pointed to the rental car pickup area. "I got it."

"Merry Christmas when it comes." He grinned at her.

"Ugh!" she groaned but then forced a smile for the man. *What is it with small-town people and this happy-go-lucky attitude every day?* It was never something she'd gotten used to— how nice everyone always was. It didn't seem like the real world.

And it didn't get any better. As soon as she passed the sign that welcomed her to Yuletide Creek, an old weather-beaten sign that read, *Welcome to Yuletide Creek, Population 10,213,* her first thought was that she wouldn't make it ten-thousand two-hundred and fourteen. Nicole had one goal only— to convince her mother to sell the shop and get back to Seattle. She was mostly there to help with her transition from it and possibly to find something else that wasn't so taxing. Or nonsensical.

The town was pretty much the same as the last time she was there. She passed the farm soon after the sign and then the gas station— a rundown, dingy place like the one you'd see in the movies. There were only two pumps, a broken-down air pump, and a convenience store to the side with the name "Sal's Sip n' Dip" painted in faded white letters.

"Howdy!" the lone car owner at the pump waved when he saw her slowing down.

"Hey," she replied and checked her gas meter. She was thinking about filling up just so she wouldn't have to come back later. But she had about a half tank. She'd fill up later when she needed it. It wasn't as if she was going to paint the town red.

So, she kept on driving until she got to the main thoroughfare. She had to pass city hall first, and she slowed down to a crawl as she gazed at it— it seemed in stark contrast to all the other buildings. It was overlaid with a brick finish set on a large lawn that she imagined was very vibrant in the spring and summer months. It had a white-picket fence at the front on either side of the stone pathway that led to the large, red oak door at the front.

"Makes sense," she said as she continued driving. She was literally getting her fill of everything she'd missed for the past twenty-four years.

But when she got to the town square, she realized she hadn't missed much after all. The stores were the same—the same diner, with probably the same waitress in the red-and-white checkered outfit, but older. The hardware store, the smoke shop, and the same paint-stripped fire hydrant in front of Owen's Grocery Store.

"Yep, some things never change," she mused to herself. "One more reason to do what I gotta do and get the heck out of here."

But, speaking of the diner. Her stomach started to rumble as she thought about the food. She hadn't eaten all morning, and it was already early afternoon. What did she have to lose? It was either that or wait for her mother to get home and make something.

"Nope, the diner will do," she said as she pulled up alongside the curb just outside the establishment.

She glanced inside and saw that it wasn't really busy. Maybe it would get that way later that evening, but for the moment, she appreciated not having to wait for her meal.

"Hello!" the perky woman behind the register hailed and gave her a bright smile. Of course, she was wearing a checkered red and white outfit. "Welcome to Yuletide Creek. How may I help?"

"Thank you," Nicole replied as her eyes scoured the menu board. "Uh, could I get the large cheeseburger with waffle fries and a strawberry lemonade, please?"

"Good choice," she said, grinning ear to ear. "We'll be with you in a few."

"Thanks." Nicole took a seat by the window.

She gazed through the smeared glass at the outside world. She felt as if she were in Oz. The people who walked by didn't seem as if they had a care in the world, always smiling and waving. Heck, maybe something was wrong with her because she didn't smile as much.

"Your order, ma'am," a young girl in the same outfit said when she got to the table.

"Oh, thanks," Nicole replied and glanced across the street at the fire hydrant. "Tell me something," she said out of sheer curiosity. "I haven't been back here in a while. I thought they'd have that fixed by now."

The girl raised her eyebrow in curiosity. "Nothing much has been fixed around here in a while, and with Mayor Luke 'the Grinch' running things, I doubt he'll spend any money on anything."

"Hmm, interesting," Nicole mused, then sipped on her drink as she kept her eyes trained outside.

"But who knows?" the girl said as she threw her hands in the air. "Maybe he'll fix it now that his grandfather is done gone and bought a brand-new fire truck."

"Wow." Nicole giggled while the girl joined in. "That makes all the sense in the world."

"Tell me about it," the waitress said and rolled her eyes. "Anyway, enjoy your meal." She hurried off to get the next order.

The cheeseburger tasted a lot better than Nicole thought it would, and she found herself devouring the greasy meal in no time. Her stomach was grateful for it. And she was more content too. Enough to see the town through new lenses.

It wasn't that bad for a town of its size. And money didn't flow into these towns as much. Maybe what they needed was a generous benefactor, some investors, or some really good fund-raising initiatives.

"Old antique store," someone said from the booth behind her, and her ears perked.

"Yeah, it's such a great little store," a woman replied excitedly. "I've found so many little trinkets there I'm not sure I'd find anywhere else."

Way to go, Mom!

"I like the displays," a little girl, probably about seven, commented. "Today, they have a Native-American village. The whole thing. With people and everything!"

"I think they do a pretty good job of changing the displays so often. It keeps the store interesting," the woman, probably the little girl's mother, told her.

"Yep, it's one of those stores you like to walk past," the supposed father chimed in. "Susie, please don't hold your cup like that."

And then, the conversation changed, and Nicole stopped listening. But she understood then what her mother's problem was— *how would she ever sell anything if she was busy having a show every day?* Nicole could bet most of the onlookers never spent a dime.

"I can't wait to see the Christmas display," the little girl added after a long while.

Aww, shoot! Nicole had forgotten, once again, that it would be Christmas soon. Her mother was probably already knee-deep in tinsel and pine. If she could ever find anything. Nicole couldn't put a damper on her spirits by trying to strong-arm her into selling the shop.

She'd wait until after Christmas.

Nicole figured she could endure that one as she'd done the others. Luckily, it was just one day, even though the festivities lasted for the entire month. But who knew? She might surprise herself.

She finished her meal and swiped her purse off the table. Nicole dodged a few of the townspeople who were curious to chitchat and find out who she was related to and how long she'd be in town. She passed the B&B a block down with a banner out front that advertised vacant rooms.

"Not surprising," Nicole muttered. The town really didn't seem as vibrant despite the attempts by the store owners to perk up the place with the festive lights. There was cracked pavement, other rundown shops, like Marty's Liquor Store, which had most of the letters missing from the name, and The Spot. Nicole wasn't sure what was being sold inside, but outside, the faded paint and lack of scenery didn't give her any clue.

Fortunately, there was only one antique store in town, so it wasn't hard for the GPS to find it. But even if she were just driving and checking out displays in the store-fronts, she couldn't have missed it. Not the life-sized Native American man out front with an ax, as if he was guarding the other miniature figurines and dolls in the glass case.

"You've got to be kidding me," she exclaimed and laughed to herself. The family in the diner hadn't been wrong. Her mother had gone all out on the display. Typical. She always went overboard with any project she took on, which explained why the store was no longer something she could manage.

Nicole shook her head and got out of the car. She was tempted to take up the life-sized figure and haul it back inside the door. Except for the fact that a red-haired teenage boy was standing next to it, posing for a photo.

Someone must be hazing him— why else would anyone want a photo? Then again, the image in the backdrop would make it look as if they were on the actual Mohican reservation.

It didn't surprise her that there were wind chimes over the door, and she stepped inside, fully expecting to see her mother in a headwrap to go with the theme. She was nowhere to be seen.

"Mom?" she called out while walking through the store. She walked by shelves loaded with trinkets, beads, boxes, candlestands, photos, keyrings, and books— it was as if she never threw anything out.

Her eyes caught something to her right. She turned to see a man moving through the space between the book-shelves. He didn't seem to have seen her, but he kept picking things up and putting them in a jacket he wore.

"Really!" she said to herself as she walked the other way so she'd come upon him from behind. She was right. He was just going through the aisle, picking up things and stuffing them into his pockets.

She cleared her throat, and he jumped, knocked his elbow against a tin lamp, toppling it, and then dived to stop it from crashing to the floor. He didn't look like a common criminal if that had a look. He was dressed in a pair of jeans with a white tee under an open-front flannel shirt. He had dark hair that was graying at the temples, which made him look rather distinguished. He could have passed for the owner of the store if she didn't know any better. Not a thief!

Nicole folded her arms and stared at him incredu-lously. "Are you sure you don't want to pocket that too?"

"What?" he asked, narrowing his eyes. "Oh, no," he replied, then started laughing.

"I don't get what's so funny about stealing worthless stuff. What kind of psycho are you?"

"Uh, I don't know," he said, then set the lamp on the shelf again. "The kind that works in the store, apparently."

At that moment, she could feel her cheeks burning crimson with embarrassment.

Chapter Three

"**O**h," Nicole replied as she flushed a bright red. "It's fine." He chuckled, a low rumble coming from his belly. "I would have thought I was a thief, too, but I'm really just looking for things that need fixing."

"Okay," she said, looking around the store, careful to avoid his gaze. It wasn't often that she was wrong, so the few times it happened, her cheeks would flush. "That makes sense, I guess."

"I'm sorry, did you want something?" he asked, squinting at her.

"Yes, I was looking for my mother," she said, looking around the store again. "God, there's a lot of stuff here."

"Your mother?" he asked, his eyebrows creasing.

"Yeah, Trisha," Nicole told him as she turned back around to him.

"Mrs. Hayes is your mother?" he asked with an incredulous look. "I see the resemblance now. I don't know how I missed it."

"Is she here?" Nicole wanted to know. She wasn't

sure what it was about him, but he seemed magnetic. It had to take extra effort not to look at him— his square jaw and that tiny dimple in his chin when he smiled. It was like ripping your eyes away from an atrocious sight, only in this case, it was more like the crowned jewel.

"She went out for a bit to get something for dinner, I think," he replied while he searched his brain. "Is there anything I can get you in the meantime?"

"I'm good, thanks. I'll just wait, I guess." She paused as she looked around for a place she could possibly wait.

"Office is back there." He pointed to a brown door to the back of the store. "Does she know you're coming?"

"Yes, thank you. I appreciate it," she said, then hurriedly walked away. He must have thought she was weird. She felt silly the way her heart was fluttering

And she couldn't walk fast enough. The hairs on the back of her neck stood on end, and she imagined him watching her walk away, making her even more self-conscious. But when she looked back, he wasn't there. She guessed it was all in her head, and a small part of her was disappointed.

A really minuscule part.

Microscopic, really.

She hummed as she walked through the small walkways between the aisles. "How does anyone find anything in here?" she mumbled to herself as she saw what looked like Aladdin's lamp. She giggled as she took it down and rubbed the sides with her sleeve. "What? No genie?" She chuckled just as the door opened, and Trisha walked in.

"Oh, you're here!" her mother exclaimed. She set the brown paper bag down on the glass-top counter, then hurried over to her. Her long, brown hair with streaks of gray flowed from underneath the black wool hat she wore.

It was a perfect match to the pair of black jeans, which she wore with a gray sweatshirt and a black puffer jacket. "Give your mom a hug," she said, then pulled Nicole into a fierce embrace.

"Uh, you're choking the life out of me," Nicole croaked and wrapped her arms around her. She wasn't sure how she would feel seeing her mother again, but she didn't expect the warm, fuzzy feeling inside and the feeling of familiarity.

"Sorry, honey. I'm just so glad to see you." She smiled. "Where's Stevie?"

"She can't come until her exams are done mid-December," Nicole told her. "So, for now, all you have is me."

"I'm good with that," she quipped, taking a step back to grip Nicole's forearms and grinning like a Cheshire cat. "I am just swelling up inside right now."

"Okay." Nicole laughed, but even though she did, she still couldn't shake the guilt over why she'd left town in the first place. "You went out," she said, glancing over at the counter where her mother had left the bags. "What did you get?"

"Oh, just some spices. I thought I'd make your favorite," she said with a wink.

"Roast beef?" Nicole asked excitedly, feeling like a teenager again.

"You got it." Trisha returned, pulling the scarf from around her neck. "This is a special occasion."

"Not that I don't appreciate it, but you didn't have to do that," Nicole returned as she feigned humility.

Trisha laughed. "I can always make something else." Trisha raised her brows, taunting Nicole with it.

"Roast beef is perfect." She snickered, and Trisha

joined in her laughter. Then a moment of awkward silence followed before Nicole cleared her throat and looked around. "So, the shop. It has a lot of stuff."

"Yep," Trisha said. "A whole lot. I'm swimming in it."

"More like drowning," Nicole shot, spreading her arms. She reached over and picked up an eighteen-inch bronze fork from the shelf closest to her. "Who's gonna buy this? A witch with a large cauldron?"

Trisha laughed and snatched the fork from her. "It can make a nice wall accessory in a kitchen. I have the matching spoon too."

Nicole groaned as she surveyed the store. "When you said you needed help, I didn't think you needed an army."

"Oh, it's not so bad. I just need to get everything organized, that's all," she replied cheerily. "Like the fork and spoon should be together. Things like that."

Nicole watched the way her face lit up when she spoke. She felt like a hypocrite— she knew she wasn't there to help to catalog anything. She'd make a show of it, but what she really wanted to do was convince her mother to sell the shop. From the looks of things, it was going to be a daunting task.

"Okay, give me a few minutes to lock the office, and we'll get out of here," Trisha said and patted Nicole's arm. "So excited."

Nicole smiled as her mother walked off. She walked around the shop as she waited. She was pretty sure she saw a dinosaur bone. And the first pot a caveman ever made.

"Mom, you really need to just get rid of some of this stuff," she was forced to say when Trisha returned.

"Someone might want it," Trisha returned stubbornly as they went through the door.

"Like who? Wilma Flintstone? People are more into contemporary things now, not ancient pottery and creepy vases."

"Sweetie, can we not talk about that now? I want to hear everything about you and your job—your life. And are you dating anyone?"

"Mom, you know that's not happening. Rudy was a jerk, and I'm not in a hurry to have a relationship with anyone." She sighed. "I'll follow you to the house," she said, ending that conversation before it picked up traction. Dating was the last thing she wanted to think about.

"All right. I'm just up the street." Trisha pointed, then hurried away.

Nicole got into her car and pulled off the curb after her mother drove off. The quaint little town was coming to life at dusk, and the lights in the storefronts came on one by one. She could feel the Christmas spirit trickling into Yuletide Creek, and once again, her heart sank.

They passed some well-lit homes with Santa Claus and reindeer props on lawns, sleighs on roofs, and pine trees covered with lights and candy canes in several yards. She didn't see much of this where she lived in Seattle but peering out of her window at the houses already decked out for Christmas, she couldn't help but feel a tinge of the holiday spirit.

The house was just as she remembered— three-foot, white picket fence, green shrubbery on the inside, and flowerpots, now devoid of trees nestled against the stone walkway that led to the stone stoop. There weren't any hanging flower pots like the last time she'd left, but the rocking chair and porch swing were still there— mementos of her childhood.

"Well, don't just stand there," Trisha urged, wiping

her feet on the "Merry Christmas" welcome mat. The white door showcased a red-and-green wreath with a ribbon across the front that matched the words on the mat.

And inside was just as she remembered— spotless. The floorboards were like glass, and a runner stretched from the door to the archway that led to the living room. Nicole felt like a stranger in the house where she grew up.

"It's been so long. It feels weird being back," she admitted, mostly to herself, as memories of that fateful night bombarded her subconsciousness, and a fresh wave of guilt followed. She had no right to be there. Her place wasn't in Yuletide Creek anymore.

"This visit is long overdue. And I hope you know you'll always have a home here."

Nicole felt as if she couldn't be more wrong.

When she walked upstairs to her old room, everything was just as she'd left it, except for the bedsheets. Her nightstand with the heart-shaped night-light was still there, the stickers on her closet mirror, and her graduation photo on the chest.

"Oh," she gasped when she saw the stuffed dog her boyfriend had given her back then. She picked it up and started turning it over.

"I thought you might want to keep that," Trisha said from the doorway.

"Why? You hated Aaron."

"I didn't hate him," Trisha replied, then rocked her head from side to side. "You were only fifteen."

"Yeah, I didn't get better at boys, did I?" She sighed.

"Don't do that to yourself," Trisha chided, then walked over to her, clasping her face in her palms. "Rudy didn't deserve you, and what happened wasn't your fault."

"I know." Nicole sighed again.

"So how about you wash up, and I'll make you a plate, huh?"

"Thanks, Mom," Nicole said.

The shower actually did her some good. She felt as if she'd just washed the weight of the world off herself and was ready for what would come next. Except she wasn't. She couldn't get over the fact that maybe she was just good at ruining relationships, and that was why her own marriage didn't last.

Trisha had slices of the roast beef carved already, along with mashed potatoes, garlic-butter green beans, and asparagus covered in parmesan cheese.

"Wow. Who's all this food for? Are there more people coming over?" Nicole asked as she sat. Her mind still wasn't right, but the shower did her some good.

Trisha laughed. "You know my hands have always been heavy when it comes to food. I could never cook anything for less than five people."

"So, you've basically wasted a whole lot of food, or you've been feeding the town," Nicole quipped, then spooned some mashed potatoes into her mouth.

"More like feeding the town," she admitted. "People have popped in from time to time."

"I can totally see that happening," Nicole replied, then helped herself to the green beans. "We always had visitors, even when I was growing up."

"Yeah, we did." Trisha smiled.

They ate in silence for a couple of minutes before Nicole exhaled. "Mom, why did you even get the shop in the first place? And why do you keep getting new things."

Trisha blew a breath out and used her hand to sweep her hair back. "You know, ever since your father left, and then you, roughly a year later, I was on my own. I had no one. Nothing. I had to find a way to deal and keep busy, so I started the shop. I've been doing it ever since. It's all I have."

Well, crap!

Nicole's heart cracked in two. She felt awful for thinking badly about the shop. She'd been the one to leave right after her parents got divorced because she couldn't bring herself to stay. When she was seventeen, she'd gone out in her parents' Bronco and had wrecked it. It caused a huge argument between her parents that night, and Nicole couldn't say for sure that they ever made up afterward. Until one day, her father just left.

If she hadn't done what she did, they'd still be together. And then she'd left her mother too. "I'm sorry, Mom. It's just that— it's a lot of things, and I don't think you need all of it!"

"I know, but I just need to get it all sorted. That's all. Once you help me with that, I'll be able to manage better."

They resumed eating in silence for the most part after. Nicole was saddened by her mother's loneliness, and she could sense that Trisha wasn't sure what to say to her sometimes.

"How about a game of cribbage?" Trisha asked when she was finished clearing the table.

"Wow, I haven't played that in a long time," Nicole admitted. "Let's go."

"All right, then."

They washed the dishes together before Trisha got the board and laid it out on the coffee table in the living room. They were halfway through their first game when Trisha's eyes lit up.

"So, I see you met Jake," she beamed.

"Ugh, get it out of your head. I didn't come here for you to play matchmaker," Nicole dismissed her and focused on her next move.

"Well, he is a sweetheart. I don't know what I would have done without him. He does the groceries for me sometimes, opens up the shop and does the display, works the register, and then comes over to help with the gardening or anything I need. I tell you, he's a catch."

"So, you reel him in. You wouldn't be the first cougar around town," Nicole joked.

Trisha laughed. "Maybe the only one in Yuletide Creek. I'd probably get shunned for that."

"I don't know. I didn't have such a great impression of him," Nicole admitted, looking at her mother across the table.

"That's because you don't know him. Yet," she wagged her brows at her daughter.

"Forget it, Mom," Nicole told her.

"Well, at least he's better than your no-good ex, even if you don't believe me," she insisted.

But with that, Nicole silently agreed.

No one could have been worse than Rudy.

And she had the battle scars to prove it.

Chapter Four

Nicole woke up the following morning feeling like a stranger in her body and in a new world. She was displaced when she opened her eyes, looked at the floral wallpaper, and heard the bed creak when she moved.

And then she remembered— she wasn't at home back in Seattle in her usual bed. She was in Yuletide Creek, her childhood home. She temporarily questioned her return. All it had done so far was remind her of why she'd left. She was experiencing the same emotions that had driven her out of town in the first place, and it was slowly taking root.

But then, if she wasn't there, she'd have been sliding down the corridor to the copy room for an ingrate.

When she considered the alternative, Yuletide Creek didn't seem so bad. Warts and all.

She rolled out of bed and walked with half-opened eyes to the bathroom. The cold water she unwittingly splashed on her face was enough to wake her up.

"Shoot!" she said as she grabbed the green towel from

the bar. She'd forgotten that the hot water was on the wrong side. The plumber had installed it wrong so many years ago, and her mother hadn't bothered to fix it.

But she was awake nevertheless, and her rumbling stomach punctuated the thought. She clapped her hand on it and spoke to it like a child. "Fine, I'll get something to eat. Sheesh!"

"You're awake," her mother asked when she made her way into the kitchen. Trisha was standing by the kitchen island reading the morning paper.

"Morning, Mom. What time does the shop open?"

She stopped reading to check the time. "Uh, at nine. It's only minutes past seven now. We have some time."

"Okay," Nicole replied and wandered over to the fridge. "Do you have coffee?"

"No," her mother told her. "I have tea if you'd like that."

"Tea?" Nicole turned, echoing the word while still bent over in front of the fridge.

"What's wrong with tea?" her mother asked with a laugh.

"Nothing," Nicole said. "I'll have to get some. And probably a pot. Oh, wait, maybe you have an original coffee mortar in the shop. I could grind it myself."

"Very funny. You keep mocking my store. Wait until you see the treasures that lie within." Trisha winked at her mysteriously.

"Can't wait," Nicole responded sarcastically and grabbed the bottle of orange juice. "Guess I'm going light this morning. Don't blame me if I get cranky. This isn't my usual morning routine."

"It's just for one morning. You'll get over it," Trisha replied. "Maybe we can go into the store early to get a head start. There's a lot of work to do. And later, we can start putting up the lights and decorating the tree."

"Hey, hold your horses," Nicole said as she stood. "One challenge at a time. Plus, a Christmas tree? Is it really necessary?"

"Of course it is," Trisha said resolutely.

"Why?" Nicole asked, gazing at her mother with an arched eyebrow.

"It's Christmas, or have you forgotten what Christmas in Yuletide Creek is like?"

"That's a distinct possibility." Nicole nodded, then downed her juice. But even after nearly twenty-five years, the wounds she carried were still fresh. Time had done nothing to assuage her shame. Christmas wasn't making her feel happy. It was giving her anxiety, but she didn't want to dampen her mother's mood. She could do that one thing for her.

"You know what? I can do that," Nicole replied, setting her glass down on the counter. "I have nothing else to do."

"Great." Trisha grinned and hurried off. "Be right back. I'm going to freshen up. I can't wait to get started on the tree. When Stevie comes, she's going to love it," she shouted from the stairs.

Nicole thought it would be good if she freshened up too. By eight, they were both ready. But what Nicole wasn't ready for was the chaos.

"I don't know how you function in this," she said as she turned around in the antique junkyard.

"There's a method to my madness," Trisha told her, then patted her arm.

"That, or just madness," Nicole grunted in response.

"Come on." Her mother chuckled.

She followed her into the tiny office, which had even more trinkets. Nicole shook her head and set her purse down on the worn desk. Paper was strewn all over it, and a single laptop remained closed.

"Do you even use this?" she asked her mother.

"I do. Jake helps sometimes, but who knows how to really use these things?" she asked and waved Nicole off.

"I guess I need to literally start at the top. With a notepad. Do you have one?"

Trisha slid the desk drawer open. "Yes, I have one here."

"And a pen," Nicole added as she took up the notepad. "I can see my day is going to be awesome." She grinned.

"Why do you always have to be so sarcastic?" Trisha laughed.

"Can't help it." Nicole shrugged. "It's my only charm."

She walked out of the office and stood in one of the aisles, scratching her head. She didn't know where to start. Or what to start with. Or how to start. *Should I sort by size? Pricing? Like items?* There weren't even any prices.

"Mom!" she called out.

"Yes?" Trisha replied, poking her head through the door.

"Do you have a price gun or something you can price with?"

"Uh, no, but I think Paul has them down at the hardware store," she told her.

Nicole thought about it, but she didn't want to make a supply run just yet— she might need more items. So, she decided she'd just start labeling. "Do you have labels?" Nicole shouted again.

"No!" her mother told her, sounding exasperated.

Nicole threw her hands in the air and walked back to the office. "So, you're literally running a flea market in a store?"

"People come in, look around, and pick up stuff they like. Then they ask me how much, and I give them a price," she explained, then shrugged as if it was the simplest process in the world. "I didn't think I needed to label anything."

"Yes," Nicole said with understanding. "Maybe because you don't even know what to call half of these things."

"That's sometimes true, but people don't care. They like it. They'll buy it. Name or no name."

"Well, if I'm going to get this shop organized, I'll need to know prices, and I need labels, so later, I'll get a price gun from Paul's. At least that." She was rethinking the labeling. It would be too much to go through labeling all those items and then price them.

That was when she decided that was the best course of action— grouping them according to prices. So, she got to work. She walked to the back of the store and busied herself organizing the shelves. She was so caught up in her task that she didn't realize how quickly the time was going until she turned and almost ran into Jake.

"Hey," she greeted, then caught her breath. "I didn't know you were here."

"Yeah, I've been in my own corner. I saw you were busy, so," he commented. He was chewing on a toothpick, which gave him a rugged yet charming look that triggered her heart rate. The pair of black jeans he wore was faded, and he wore a navy sweatshirt that was rolled up to his elbows, revealing smooth lines of hair on his forearm.

"Okay. What time is it?" Nicole asked, then wiped the sweat from her brow.

"Half past noon," he replied casually.

"Really? Wow, I need to get something to eat. I'll have to come back to this. Nearly four hours have flown by, and I'm still on the back shelf."

He chuckled. "Why do you think I never bothered with it?"

"Ugh!" she groaned, then walked off. "Be right back." She made her way to the front of the store, where her mother stood behind the cash register.

"Mom, I'm going to grab something to eat and then pick up those items I need. Do you want anything?"

"Yes, that would be lovely," she said as she pulled out the cash register. "I'm out of tape."

"Okay, I'll get that. Do you want anything to eat?"

"No, thanks. I'm good."

"All right. Be back in a jiffy," Nicole said and walked outside. The air was getting pretty nippy, and she lowered her head as she hurried for the car. She decided to get the items she needed before getting lunch. By then, her stomach was in knots.

She passed a local eatery, The Roasted Bean, which piqued her interest. "Can't be that bad," she told herself as she parked and got out of the car. Several people were milling about, and the shop next door, a jewelry store, was busy setting up its Christmas display. So far, they had snowdrops sprayed onto the glass window, and Santa was swaying inside while ringing a bell. Two men were outside trying to get the lights up along the front and in the corners.

She walked into the eatery and found that it had more patrons than the diner. They had an interesting menu, which resulted in her ordering a black bean, spicy salsa, and mushroom chicken wrap. Yeah, it was as weird as it sounded, but it tasted great.

She dug into what was probably her tenth bite when she noticed the gentleman at the bar area staring at her. She paused in the middle of her eating, narrowed her eyes, and then looked away. That had not been enough — her gaze must have been enough to garner his attention.

"Hey," he said from right next to her.

"Hello," she replied, looking up at him. He was a well-dressed man with messy, blond hair that looked as if he belonged on Wall Street— suit and all. "Can I help you?"

"I just saw you over here looking lonely and wondered if you needed company," he explained, then sat.

Her jaw almost dropped at his abruptness. He didn't even wait for her invitation. "Don't mind me. Feel free to sit," Nicole shot, narrowing her eyes at him.

He chuckled. "The name's Alan, and I'm just in town for the holidays. Are you a native?"

She thought about not answering him at all. He'd been rude, and she didn't want to encourage him, but something told her he didn't need an external source. "No, I'm from out of town too."

"I knew it," he said proudly as if he'd just bet on a winning horse. "I knew something as pretty as you couldn't belong here."

Something?

Nicole didn't bother to respond. She went right on

eating before he ruined her appetite. That was inevitable. "Did you come for the Christmas festivities too?"

"You're here for that?" She had to ask because he looked nothing like the type that fancied reindeer and fat guys in red suits.

"Well, don't say it like that." He laughed. "I happen to like Christmas. Don't let the suit fool you."

"Hard not to," Jake said from her right. She hadn't even seen when he'd come in.

"Jake, are you following me?" she asked.

He smirked and held up the cup of coffee in his hand. "I came for this. Didn't know you'd be here with your friend."

"He's not my friend," she replied, her face starting to flush.

"Excuse me, but we're trying to have a conversation," Alan retorted, clearly upset that he'd been interrupted.

"So am I," Jake told him.

Nicole clenched her jaw at Jake's rudeness. She got up and grabbed his hand. "Can you please give these to my mother," she requested, then crossed her arms.

He looked intently at her, then at the man before he took the bag and walked out.

"Small-town hicks," Alan commented after Jake was gone. "I could never live here."

"Yeah, you wouldn't fit in," Nicole replied hotly. He was much too arrogant for anywhere but the moon.

And her appetite was officially lost. "Look, I have to get back to the store. Nice talking to you, Alan."

"You too...?" he drawled as he waited for her to tell him her name.

"It's Nicole," she said, then shook his unusually soft hands.

"Nice to meet you, Nicole." He grinned at her. *The pleasure was all yours.* "Maybe I'll see you at another, more convenient time."

Uh, not a chance!

She shook her head and got up. But he'd thrown her off, and Jake had been weird. Nicole hadn't parked far from the store, so she figured she'd go for a walk and clear her head before she dove into more odd, dusty items she'd grow intimate with over the next couple of days.

Her walk took her past the Yuletide Creek Library, and like many of the other shops, it too had its own exhibit. But it wasn't all about Christmas, which sparked her curiosity, so she stopped to check it out.

There were two displays— one was a winter-themed art project put together by the town's elementary children, which was on the left side of the store, and on the right, there was a brief history of Yuletide Creek.

She walked inside to get a better look and started to read through one of the info strips. According to it, Yuletide Creek was founded as a logging and milling ocean-side town. Back in the early days, over a hundred years ago, a forest fire had wiped out an entire section of the town— along the street where the library stood. Many of the town's original records were lost in the fire at city hall, which was originally on Main Street.

She narrowed her eyes and looked at the picture of the old city hall. It looked somewhat familiar.

"This display always attracts the tourists," someone said from behind her. "Hi, I'm Jean, the librarian," a woman with a pixie cut said as she introduced herself.

"This is very interesting. I grew up here, but I don't remember this," Nicole replied.

"That's not strange. Many people don't know the

history of the town. It doesn't help that it's almost like a legend now, considering memories have faded, and there's nothing to back anything up."

"Wow," Nicole said. "So, it's almost like discovering an entire new world."

Jean laughed. "Something like that. But everything you see here on Main Street was built in the last century, after what they called The Great Blaze. It's interesting that this town was a milling and logging town. We hardly do any of that anymore. Not since that fire. It chased everyone out of town. It wasn't until later that we started doing fishing charters, expeditions, and other things that attracted some tourism, but you still have a few men who mill lumber. The Bryans over on Collins Street."

"Well, thank you for that bit of info. That was really informative. The things you learn," Nicole said.

"Oh, this town isn't short on stories, but you'd have to come back for history night to hear the rest," she said as she extended the invitation, and Nicole took the pamphlet she offered.

"Thanks, Jean. It was nice meeting you," Nicole said as she made her way back outside.

As Nicole walked back to her car, she wondered how many other secrets the town held that were lost in the fire — the things no one would ever know again.

Chapter Five

If Nicole had realized what she was getting into, she'd have probably chosen to stick it out with Dr. Anthony instead.

What she'd expected to be an enormous task had morphed into an impossible one. It was day three, and she was still trying to organize the back shelf. It didn't help that her mother kept bringing new things in. She had no clue where she kept finding antique items to add.

"Mom!" Nicole cried, flustered one day when her mother hauled in a wooden rocking horse. "Really?"

"What?" she asked innocently. "Some child could use this. And it's almost Christmas. I bet this one will go in a jiffy."

"Where do you keep getting these things?" Nicole asked, feeling the frustration already sinking in. "Is there an antique junkyard in town I don't know about?"

Her mother chuckled. "Here and there," she quipped, then walked back to the cash register to handle a customer who had a music box in their hand.

How in the world does she keep track of sales?

Someone could just walk in, take something and go, and she'd never even know it.

She chuckled at the thought of someone stealing anything from the shop. They'd be doing her a favor at that point. *Or maybe people don't steal in Yuletide Creek. Maybe that only happens in downtown Seattle.*

She was on the verge of losing her mind. It was as if her mother never threw anything out. She was a hoarder, and they weren't just large items. Or even medium-sized. There were tons of trinkets, jewelry, household items, paintings, murals, mugs, coffee pots, and chamber pots— what was anyone going to do with a chamber pot from the days of pit latrines?

She placed her notepad on the shelf and rubbed her temples. She'd never get it all done. Not when she was doing it alone. Her mother wasn't helping. And then there was Jake. She glanced to where he now stood, covered in decorations and painstakingly arching his body to get that last snowdrop in the right place on the window display.

She sucked in a deep breath and walked over to him. Nicole could feel her annoyance mounting. It was as if she was the only one in the store who cared about order.

She crossed her arms and started tapping her feet on the ground when Jake turned and noticed her. "Can I help you with something?" he asked, his brows dipping as he did.

"As a matter of fact, yes!" she exclaimed, spreading her arms out. "Help with this."

"Hey, you've got your job, and I've got mine," he replied, picking up an elf from off the ground.

"But don't you think I'd go faster if I had a little help?" she asked, feeling as if she was being tormented.

He pointed to the display. "Ditto."

Nicole grunted. "What's with changing the display every single day? Can't you have one display for the season like everyone else?" she asked furiously as her hands fell to her side in defeat.

"We're not like everyone else." He grinned, completely ignoring the fact that she was getting angry. It was hard to ignore the way the muscles in his arms rippled with each movement or how his clean-shaven face gave him a boyish charm that was working its way into her system— a charm she tried desperately to ignore.

"Clearly!" she snapped. "Other people throw things out."

He chuckled. "You know, despite the way it looks, there is some order to all of this chaos."

"You don't say," she groaned just as her eyes started twitching. "Since you're clearly familiar with this order, don't you think it would make a lot more sense for you to be helping me instead of constantly setting up window displays?"

"Well, this is my job, and that is yours," he replied, his gaze meeting hers. "If I had help finishing my job, I'd be free to help you with yours."

"Why can't you help me with mine first?" she asked, and as soon as she asked the question and saw his raised brows, she realized how dumb it sounded.

"Because mine can be finished today," he said.

It was as if he was mocking her. She grunted, shook her head, and threw her hands in the air. "Fine. Let's just get this over with."

"See that now? Teamwork."

"Whatever," she grumbled. "What am I doing?"

"You can hold this end of the lights right here while I

attach this on the other wall," he told her. She did as she asked and watched as he climbed up the step ladder to hook one end to the far right of the display window.

"I don't even know why people get so all worked up during Christmas. It's just one day," Nicole complained. Then she realized she'd said that out loud, and she glanced up at Jake, hoping he hadn't heard her. She didn't want him to see how much of a scrooge she really was.

As if his opinion of her mattered.

"Me neither," he replied, climbing back down the steps.

"Huh?" she asked as her brows furrowed.

"I mean, I don't get the festivities and the whole town tree lighting thing and whatnot," he told her as he walked over to her side and took the other end of the lights from her.

His hand brushed against hers, and she felt goose pimples running up and down her neck and spine. It was easy for her to get a whiff of his musky scent, and immediately her mind started replaying the last time she'd been with a man. When she glanced up, he was staring at her, and when their eyes locked, her throat instantly felt dry. *What is with my stupid body?*

She quickly looked away and hoped he wasn't still staring. "So, you don't like Christmas either?" she rubbed the back of her neck.

"Uh, yes and no," he replied, then started unwrapping little elves that were kept in a shoe box. "Put these there," he indicated a faux pine bedding.

"Yes and no?" she asked curiously. "How come?"

"Well, I've never had much to do with the whole thing, but I like making people happy, and Christmas seems to make people happy, so," he said and spread his arms.

"Oh, I see," she said as a smile tore her lips apart. She hadn't expected that answer from him, but she was impressed by it. "That's very admirable."

"Yeah, it is what it is," he stated.

She felt as if his response had cast a shadow over her already dark demeanor. She wished she could be as selfless as he was, but she wasn't there yet. Christmas for her still represented pain and loss.

It didn't take more than an hour for them to finish with the display, so she was ecstatic when Jake was finally able to help her with organizing the shop.

"This feels like it's going much faster," she said as she cataloged some trinkets. "But if it were up to me, I'd throw out half of this stuff." She turned around to make an example. She picked up what looked like an eighteenth-century frock. "Like this. What in blazes is this?"

His eyes widened. "Are you kidding me? You only talk like this because you don't know the history behind this," he bragged.

She crossed her arms. "Like what? Someone got tired of it and threw it out?"

He shook his head in disbelief. "That's a tartan, for your information, and is very valuable, especially around Halloween time. Do you know that this belonged to an actual Scottish Highlander? Huh? Bet you didn't know that. Lord of the Mackenzie clan came here over fifty years ago with his daughter. She wore this but traded it in for some local garb. She donated it to the town when she was leaving as a token of their hospitality. That was probably the only royalty we've had in town."

"Hmm," Nicole mused. "Someone knows their history."

"I bet you'd look super sexy in this thing. But you'd need a shift to go with it."

Nicole giggled at his sarcasm. The dress seemed to be made of yards of fabric. He wouldn't even be able to tell if she were a man or a woman underneath it.

"What's a shift?" she asked.

"The slip they wore under their garments," he explained as if she was the dumbest person in the world. "Don't you wear slips?" he asked, and they both burst into laughter.

"Come on, Jake. You're beginning to slow me down. Let's just focus, okay? I don't want to be here until the shop closes."

He chuckled. "Okay," he replied as they moved along the items on the back wall. Nicole picked up a dusty sword with fake jewels on the helm.

"All right, come on," she said as she picked it up. "This can go in the dump."

"Hey," Jake took the sword from her. "This once belonged to a Spanish conquistador," he explained as he wielded it, knocking over a pan from the shelf behind him.

Nicole couldn't help laughing. "Lucky you weren't on that ship."

"Very funny. I actually know how to use this," he said, then jumped back as he aimed the sword at her. "En garde!"

"I think you're mixing up your swords. That's a command used in fencing."

He stood upright again and scratched his head. "This still belonged to a Spanish conquistador."

Nicole rolled her eyes. "I think you're just making this stuff up as you go. You're no better than my mom. You're a hoarder."

"A purveyor of fine arts," he quipped, then bowed slightly.

"Yeah, right. I guess everyone can justify their madness," she returned, walking off. "Oh, what is this?" Nicole asked as something of interest caught her eye. She picked up an old jewelry box that had intricate carvings on the outside.

"That's the thing that got your attention?" he asked, waving her off.

"What? This didn't belong to Queen Elizabeth or something?"

He snickered. "Now, who's being funny?"

Nicole smiled and turned the box around in her hand. "I like it," she said.

"See? That's the same reaction we get from customers who walk in here. You don't know you want it until you see it," he said proudly, as if he'd just made his case as to why everything in the shop was necessary. "But that's nothing special, though. Those are a dime a dozen. Probably have a couple of them in here," he said nonchalantly.

Nicole opened it. The thing was well-crafted and once had a nice inlay. But even though it was sort of bent out of shape and the wood carvings were swollen, she was still fascinated by it. "I think I'll keep this one."

"Suit yourself," Jake told her.

They went through another shelf before Nicole called it quits. "Okay, I think I'm done."

"All right," Jake said and set a vial he'd been holding back on the shelf. "Same time, same place tomorrow?" He grinned.

She couldn't believe his boyish charm was working on her. "I guess so."

"Great," he replied, walking off.

Nicole picked up the jewelry box and returned to the small office with it. She'd managed to carve out her own space, and she decided to use the jewelry box as a stationery holder. She couldn't see herself putting jewelry in it, but it looked too decent to throw out.

She was getting ready to leave when her phone rang. She picked it up and saw that it was Stevie, and instantly, her heart swelled.

"Hi, honey," she beamed as she picked up her purse. "Mom, see you later," she called to her mother as she headed out the door.

"Okay, honey," Trisha called back from the cash counter.

"How's it going over there in the boondocks?" Stevie teased with a laugh.

"Very funny, but it isn't as bad as I thought it would be," Nicole confessed.

"Yeah, right." Stevie laughed. "I can bet Grandma is over there driving you nuts with that antique shop. It must be hell for you being in all that clutter. You couldn't even stand it when I didn't fix my work desk in my bedroom."

Nicole chuckled and slipped into the driver's seat of her vehicle. "You called it. It's insane the things she wants to keep. Half of the store needs to go. And to make matters worse, she has this guy, Jake, constantly changing the store window displays. And by constantly, I mean every day!"

"Ouch!" Stevie replied. "Sucks for you."

"You have no idea. He forced me into helping him set up the Christmas display this morning."

Stevie burst into laughter. "You? Making Christmas display? I would pay good money to see that."

"I know, right?" Nicole snickered, easing the car onto the street.

"I called it, though," Stevie gloated. "Those postcard towns tend to transform people. Before you know it, you'll be out caroling at each house on the block."

"No way!" Nicole protested. "I'm not that far gone."

"Ten bucks it happens," Stevie goaded her.

"You're on, missy," Nicole said, accepting the challenge, much to Stevie's amusement.

But even as she agreed, she knew she'd already lost. Yuletide Creek was already rubbing off on her. Or was it Jake?

Chapter Six

"This is ridiculous," Nicole grumbled to herself as Jake chuckled nearby.

"What's this?" a red-haired woman with a bubbly personality asked. She had a floral scarf draped over her head and around her shoulders and was holding something Nicole couldn't identify.

"Jake?" she prompted.

"Ah, that's an English pipe," he told her, smiling broadly.

"Oh," she replied excitedly. "This would do nicely for my Edward," she said, clasping the thing tightly as she moved on, surveying other items on the shelves.

She wasn't alone. Ever since the shop opened, there had been a steady stream of both tourists and locals dropping in to gawk at the store display. And once inside the store, they just had to see what was new that might interest them. Which meant Nicole wasn't getting much cataloging done, and it was driving her up the wall.

"I knew we shouldn't have done this silly display," she grumbled.

"Are you kidding?" Jake demanded. He was leaning against the back wall, looking like one of the display items that would go quickly in a flash sale. She'd definitely take him home. "Why do you think we do it? For this very reason. You know," he said, pushing himself off the wall to walk over to her. Her breath caught in her throat when he stood in front of her. "One other way of getting rid of these things is by selling them."

She stared at him with her best poker face. "We won't be able to track anything if we don't know what we have."

"Okay, how about this? Let's take the day off, get your mind off this."

"Oh yeah?" she asked. "By doing what? The work isn't gonna do itself?"

"Who knows? Maybe by the time we get back, Miss Hayes would have sold half of the items."

She giggled at his response. "I wish."

"The tree lighting ceremony is today," he said with a glint in his eye. "We could go together and check it out."

"Me?" she asked with raised brows.

"Yes, you!" he replied emphatically. "You're a person, aren't you?"

She cocked her head to the side. "Jake, that's not my thing."

"It doesn't have to be your thing. It's something to do, and clearly, you aren't getting much done here," he returned, chin-nodding at three other customers who'd just walked in.

"You're surely not making me feel any better," she said in defeat.

"So, how about it? We could get something to eat, check out the displays, and see how a tree is formally lit."

She laughed. "You make it sound so endearing."

"Is that a yes?" he asked, wagging his brows.

How could I ever say no to him?

"Fine!" she replied, throwing her hands in the air. "But if I hate it, you owe me. And I probably will."

He laughed. "Don't count me out yet."

They ended up at the diner she'd stopped at when she first arrived in town. A cheeseburger sounded just as good to her as it did then, and Jake ordered the same.

"At least I'll enjoy this," she said as she bit into the burger.

"I don't know," he said, swallowing the bite he'd already taken. "I thought the job of the Grinch was already taken. It seems he has competition."

Nicole gave him another of her famous poker stares. "Huh?"

"Mayor Luke," he explained. "He's our original Grinch. Hates Christmas as much as you do and refuses to spend a dime on anything."

"Yeah, well, maybe he has his reasons," Nicole said, then drank some of her juice.

"Figured you'd say something like that." He chuckled.

"Well, it's not like *you* like Christmas either," she pointed out.

"I'm indifferent. There's a difference. I don't poke a hole in other people's celebrations. *You,* on the other hand..."

"I don't poke a hole into anything. I'm going to that tree thing, aren't I?" she asked defensively.

"Very reluctantly, I might add," Jake replied as he finished his last bite. He glanced outside and watched as a little girl in a fur coat clutched her mother's arm and skipped along. "Look at that?"

"That's not strange," Nicole protested. "I see that all

the time. Where do you think I'm from? Under a rock?" He laughed at her words. "I just...don't like this time of year," she admitted as her voice dipped.

When she looked up, he was looking at her with piercing eyes as if he was searching her soul. "Understood," he said, rubbing his hands together. "Are you done? I don't want you to miss out on this."

"Ugh," she groaned as she got up.

"Hold on," he said as he scooted out of the booth seat and dashed to the cashier. She met him at the door carrying two cups of hot cocoa, and he handed one to her.

"Just what the doctor ordered," she said, instantly taking a sip.

"There should be a hot cocoa stand somewhere near the tree, but I love this one," he said as he held the door for her.

The cold air sliced across her face as she stepped outside. "Wow. It's cold."

He glanced up as light flakes started raining down upon them. "Yep. But this isn't so bad. I think all we'll get is flurries."

"I hope so. I'm not ready for full-on snow just yet," she confessed, pulling her coat closer around her.

"I'm not a sucker for Christmas, but tell me you don't feel different at this time of year." He spread out his arms. "I mean, smell that air," he said, sucking in a lungful of the pine and woodsy essence that wafted through the air.

"Okay, fine," she relented. "I'm into the cinnamon cookies and eggnog, but I'm not fully sold yet," she lamented.

"Soon." He grinned. "Let the reorientation begin."

She couldn't help but feel like a child next to Jake as they strolled down Main Street to the place where they would have the tree lighting. Streams of people were heading in the same direction, red and green scarves flapping in the wind, the snowflakes lightly grazing cheeks and eyes, and she watched with amusement as a little girl stood with her mouth open and tongue stretched out to catch some of the flakes as they fell.

Display cases revealed nativity scenes, with baby Jesus in swaddling clothes in a manger in one window and Santa Claus and the elves in the other. Lights hung from the shop awnings, some like waterfalls, and others with colored, running lights that chased each other around the glass cases.

"Come on, Mom! Hurry!" a little girl with a ponytail that swished down her back cried. "Or we'll miss it."

"We won't, sweetie," she told the little girl and then rolled her eyes at us. "You'd think she's never seen a Christmas tree before."

"This one is bigger than a house," she cried excitedly.

Nicole beamed at them as the mother hurried after the child, but she couldn't help feeling a little bit of the buzz. There was something about Christmas in Yuletide Creek that made even the air smell differently. She didn't have those sentiments back home. It wasn't something she'd easily get back in Seattle, considering she never really got out.

Christmas was always a time to sit in front of the TV with a tub of ice cream, watching some of her favorite reruns.

"Look at that one!" Jake pointed to a display across the street— the nutcracker guard was making a motion as if it was ushering people into the store, and in the windows, lit reindeer chased each other around the display case. They weren't really moving, but the way the lights danced, it seemed they were.

"That's such a waste of time," Nicole said, shaking her head.

"What? Are you serious?" Jake asked, clearly annoyed. "That's how you get people into the store."

"Yeah, but that's all they do. They come for the lights and then go home. They don't actually buy anything," she returned, hoping he would understand her point.

"Maybe not that day, but they will eventually. Look at Mrs. Hayes' antique shop. People come in all the time because of the display case, and they end up finding something to buy."

"Still think it's a waste of time," she insisted, sipping her cocoa.

"In any case, it's a community thing. We do this, especially at this time of the year, and we attract business to town. People come here all the time for the Christmas events, which are a staple, as you should remember, since you started out here. So, it may not benefit your store directly, but it benefits the town, and then we all get some of the kickback. Heck, sometimes we get some rich folks down here who buy some big-ticket items, like a factory or a park. Or sponsor it."

"They should make you spokesman for the town," she replied cheekily.

He laughed. "I'd apply if Mayor Luke would pay me."

"Nicole," someone shouted her name from across the street. She stopped to see who it was that knew her name and spoke it with such familiarity. "It's Nicole, right?" he asked as he stopped in front of her.

Alan.

"Yeah," she told him, her brows cocked. "Out to see the tree?"

"Yes," he said. He was dressed in a pair of chino pants and a button-down, not very Christmassy at all. "You?"

"Kinda all dressed up for a tree lighting," Jake intercepted their conversation like he'd done the first time.

"Of course, you'd think this is dressing up." Alan smirked. "Do you only own flannel?"

"Oh, so you *were* checking me out," Jake replied mockingly.

Alan clenched his jaw and inhaled sharply. "I hope you enjoy the tree lighting. I'll see you around, Nicole," Alan said, then walked off.

"He looks like someone who'd spend some big bucks," Nicole told Jake after he'd gone.

"I don't think so. The guy rubs me the wrong way," he admitted, then shivered.

Nicole laughed. "You don't even know him," she stated as they came upon the group waiting for the tree to be lit.

"I don't have to. I've seen his type in these parts before, and they're always up to no good," he explained.

"I hope you're wrong this time," Nicole told him. She didn't particularly like Alan, but she had no reason to believe he had sinister intentions. Still, she'd prefer if he didn't keep inviting himself into her life.

"It's about that time, everyone!" a voice said over the megaphone.

"That's the Grinch," Jake whispered, and Nicole giggled.

He officially ordered the lighting, and when the lights twinkled brightly, there was thunderous applause. "It does look good. It's actually quite beautiful," Nicole commented as she watched the children gather around it and the adults as they dispersed to the various food and drink stations. It was a twenty-foot-tall tree laden with tinsel, various ornaments, pine cones, garland, and candy canes. Several large candy canes made a fence around it and what she presumed were empty gift boxes lay on faux carpeting at the base.

"Told ya," Jake boasted.

After a couple of minutes, Nicole got bored. "Okay, I think I've seen enough, and there's nothing more for us to do. We already ate, and we have coffee."

"All right," he said as he looked around. "Want to go back to the shop?"

"No, I think I'll just call it a day," she said.

"Fine," he replied. "I'll walk you to your car."

And before they were ten feet away, they heard shouts of "Fire!"

Chapter Seven

Nicole bit into her burger, which made her feel as if she was floating on a pillar of clouds. The bacon cheeseburger at the diner was so much better than what she was used to back home.

So much so that she'd become a regular.

"Can I get you anything else?" Marsha, her waitress, smiled and asked.

"The usual," she told the girl.

"Coming right up," her waitress replied. And by favorite, Nicole meant a slice of their peach cobbler pie. It was to die for.

"No wonder the tree caught on fire," an old woman said from across her. She was eating with a younger woman, possibly her daughter.

"Yeah, because he won't spend any money," the younger woman said. "Probably got the cheapest lights or plugs he could find."

Nicole glanced over, and her eyes connected with the young woman, who smiled and blushed. Their voices grew very low after that, but Nicole didn't plan on sticking around. She pulled out a twenty, prepared to pay the bill when her waitress returned with her pie and bill.

As soon as the waitress returned with the pie, she got up. "Uh, I think you forgot the bill," she told Marsha.

"No. The gentleman already paid for it."

"Okay, then take this as a tip then," she told a grateful Marsha, who pocketed the money and hurried off.

Nicole smiled, then turned to where the woman pointed, hoping to see a cheeky-faced Jake. The eyes that met her, followed by the wave, were not from someone she was hoping to find. Nicole's smile faded when she saw that it was Alan.

She walked over to his table. "Are you stalking me or something?" she asked, a bit annoyed. "You keep showing up everywhere I go."

"Oh no," he replied, looking around wildly. "Sheer coincidence."

"Three times?" she asked, as she began to get a sinking feeling in the pit of her stomach.

"I swear." He held up his hands. "I saw you come in and thought I'd be nice. Maybe you'd talk to me that way."

"Thanks, but no thanks. I can pay for my own meal," she told him and reached into her purse.

"No, that's not necessary," Alan told her as she pulled out another twenty-dollar bill. "If you leave that there, this is going to be the biggest tip this place has ever gotten on one meal. Plus, I was hoping to get into your good graces since I wanted to talk to you. I was glad when you came in."

"What do you want?" she asked, then crossed her arms. She was beginning to see what Jake had seen all along. Maybe he could be the town detective. He was good at reading people.

"Just a little chat," he said with a toothy grin. "Please, have a seat. I promise I won't bite."

Nicole was suspicious, and every alarm bell in her head was ringing. She didn't think it was a coincidence that he was always around, and she wondered how many other times he'd been lurking and she hadn't noticed. But she was in a public space, and there wasn't much he could do to her there.

Furthermore, if she listened to him one time, he might just go away.

"Fine," she said and sat.

"You're just visiting town for the holidays, you said?" he asked, then sipped from his cup. He didn't have a meal in front of him, which only led her to believe that he had ordered that single cup of juice to hide behind it.

"Yes," she told him bluntly, crossing her arms again. "So? I think we already covered that the first time you interrupted my meal."

"A feisty one. Okay." He chuckled, then wiped the corners of his mouth as he looked around suspiciously. "What about that guy that keeps showing up? Is he a relative or something?"

"Is that why you asked me over? To pry into my personal life?" she snapped. "Because if that's the case..."

"No, no," he returned, reaching out to take her hand. The daggers she flung at him made him withdraw it. "Okay, first and foremost, I'm a developer, and I'm also here, in town, to scope out the properties."

"All right," Nicole replied as her brows dipped. She wasn't sure what that had to do with her. "And?"

"I was hoping that you and your mother were interested in selling the antique shop," he confessed, then stared at her like a deer in headlights.

"So, you do know who I am," she shot. "And here I was thinking I was just another woman you met at the restaurant."

"Nothing like that," he said quickly. "It's just that I've seen you around. I didn't know who you were at the time."

"Right," she said dubiously. He was offering precisely what she'd come to town for. It was like a gift wrapped and ready for her. But something in her gut told her that Alan was being shady. "What's so special about Mom's shop?" she wanted to know.

"Nothing," he returned too quickly. "You aren't the only person I've approached."

Somehow, she doubted that. She felt as if he'd been watching just her. "No thanks," she told him and got up. "The shop isn't for sale."

She turned on her heel and left before he got a chance to say anything else to her. Maybe the shop was also growing on her, but she wasn't just going to sell it to the first buyer that came looking. If it was going to be sold, she'd select the buyer with care.

When she got back to the shop, Trisha was in a mood. She had hot apple cider on the counter and was already giggling and twirling to "Jingle Bell Rock." Nicole checked to make sure the store was closed, and she wouldn't be interrupted by her customers.

"Mom, are you drunk?" Nicole asked, then started laughing as she unwound her scarf from her neck.

"Maybe." She grinned. "Dance with me," she told Nicole, taking her hand. She turned around with her for a few beats before Nicole let her guard down.

"You know what? I think I will join you," she said, pouring a cup of hot cider. They didn't have the proper glasses, so they had to make do with coffee cups. She downed the first cup and started swaying like her mother.

The reflection of the Christmas lights bounced off the walls, and Trisha turned down the ceiling lights to get the full effect.

"I feel like I'm in a club," Trisha drawled as her tongue got too heavy.

Nicole was already feeling heady after the third cup. "Santa Baby" was being played, and both women started singing along at the top of their lungs to notes that weren't in the original song.

"Santa baby, so hurry down the chimney tonight."

It was quite a sight that Jake walked in on a couple of minutes later. He probably had his own store key. Both women were leaning against each other, crooning, or more like trying to raise the dead. He scrunched up his face and walked over to the counter.

"Oh, hi, Jake," Nicole greeted, then burped loudly. "Oops." She grinned. "Sorry."

Jake laughed. "I see someone has had too much to drink. Or should I say, someone's?"

"Nah," Trisha replied, waving him off. "Why don't you join us? There's plenty."

"I don't think so." Jake shook his head, then lifted the stool from behind the counter so he could sit on it. "Someone may need to take y'all crazy women home." He chuckled.

"Mr. No Fun," Nicole teased, even as she walked and tripped over air, falling right into Jake's arms. "All work and no play make Jake a dull boy."

"Easy there, tiger," he quipped and steadied her, even

though the look in his eyes told her he wanted her to stay where she was only sober.

She wasn't in the right state of mind to even object. She simply let him stand her up again right before she pinched him on the buttocks.

"Hey," he cried, slapping her hand away playfully.

She giggled and returned to her mother. "Come on, Mom. It's just you and me, baby," she slurred a little, then swayed her arms in the air as "I'll Be Home for Christmas" played in the background.

Nicole was oblivious to everything going on around her but the bourbon swimming in her belly and the hazy outlook that accompanied it. Jake had never looked so good to her, and she found herself thinking about him in ways she'd last thought about Rudy so long ago.

She blushed, even in her drunkenness, and channeled all her mental faculties into staying away from him.

"Okay, that's enough," Jake said after a while. "We need to get you both home." He got up and picked up the keys. "I'll have to come back for you both in the morning."

"Take us home," Nicole teased as she wobbled over to him. She was losing the challenge of reining in her primal lusts.

But a part of her knew it was more than just the alcohol talking.

Chapter Eight

"Ugh!" Nicole groaned the following morning when her eyes cracked open, and it seemed she'd fallen asleep in the sun.

Her head pounded, her eyes burned, and it was way too bright. She lay back down gently, hoping that it would wear off in a few minutes.

If anything, it had gotten worse.

Half an hour later, she'd got in the prostrate position on the bed as if she was praying to the gods for help. But her head still felt as if someone was pounding on it like African drums. She sat up robotically and turned like the evil machine in *Terminator*. She knew if she made any sudden movements, she'd have to stand still for a while until the hammering subsided.

"How much did I drink?" she mumbled to herself. She couldn't remember, and last night was very hazy in her mind. She only hoped her mother kept aspirin in the medicine cabinet.

She was working up the energy to move when her phone started ringing. Very loudly. She winced and reached for it, sliding the green button before she saw who the caller was.

"Mom?" Stevie asked on the other end.

"Stevie," Nicole replied, then winced again. "Why are you talking so loudly?"

"I'm not," she returned.

"Ugh, my head is pounding," Nicole said as she rubbed her temple with her free hand.

"Wait, Mom. Do you have a hangover?" Stevie asked, then giggled.

"Don't laugh, honey," Nicole rushed out. "I feel like my head is about to split into two."

"That's what you get when you do something dumb," Stevie scolded her. "What did you drink?"

"Mom had hot cider with bourbon," Nicole confessed. "I was in a mood."

"The heavy stuff, huh?" Stevie asked.

"Yeah," Nicole replied as she vaguely remembered falling into Jake's arms and pinching his butt. "I'm going to be so embarrassed when I see Jake today."

"Why? What happened?"

"I think I pinched his butt when I was drunk," Nicole admitted, then covered her face with her hand.

Stevie exploded into laughter. "Mom, you were really out of it," she said when she finally managed to speak again. "But who's Jake?"

"He works with Mom," Nicole replied, trying to sit upright.

"Is he hot?" Stevie asked.

"Stevie, mind your own business." Nicole laughed. "But yes, he is, if you must know."

"Oh, Mom. That's cute," she teased, which only made Nicole blush even harder. She loved how close she and

Stevie were, especially after Rudy had left. It was just the two of them, so they'd become something of best friends.

"Okay, that conversation is over. You're coming next week, right?"

"Yeah. I already booked the flight. Maybe I'll come in time to go caroling with you." She laughed.

"Don't bet on it," Nicole said. "There's only so much I'm willing to do."

"We'll see," Stevie told her. "Anyway, I have to go do this exam now. Call you later."

"Okay. Love you, sweetie."

"Love you too, Mom," she replied, then hung up.

She smiled after they ended the call. Nicole was really looking forward to seeing Stevie, especially since the last time she'd seen her was over the summer. But first things first. She had to get up, shake off her throbbing headache, and get dressed. That was a lot easier to think than to do, and she reminded herself to lay off the hot cider.

When she was finally able to move, inch by inch, to the bathroom, she celebrated when she saw the bottle. But she still needed to get downstairs for water. She gently threw on her robe and began the slow descent to the kitchen, squinting her eyes as she went.

It wasn't until she was close enough that she realized the house smelled like a bakery.

"Oh, you're up," Trisha said as she picked up a bottle of water. "You look like you need this." She chuckled.

"I do," Nicole returned gratefully. She popped the pills into her mouth and sat down on the bar stool. "How come you're skipping around like you didn't drink anything, and you were drinking even before I got there?"

Trisha chuckled softly. "I'm an old woman, dear. I've

had more practice."

"Ugh!" Nicole grunted, waving her off. "Remind me next time not to accommodate you. And what is this?"

"Oh, you don't remember. Today's the annual cookie contest up at the Christmas House," Trisha told her, then opened the oven to check her goodies.

"The Christmas House? That's still there? Miss Ruth must be what..."

"Not Miss Ruth this year, honey," Trisha stopped her. "Ruth died a couple of months ago. It's her daughter Ally who's carrying on the tradition on her behalf. And a good thing too. The town needs this. It wouldn't be Yuletide Creek without all the events Ruth had started so long ago."

"Wow," Nicole replied as she thought about it. "That must be an overwhelming job."

"I believe so," Trisha said, slipping off her mittens. "She was the only one who decorated the town tree."

"You're kidding me," Nicole said, surprise lacing her words. "That's a huge tree."

"I guess no one wanted to do it, so she did. Well, it wasn't just her. Mayor Luke helped."

"Mayor Luke? The Grinch?" Nicole asked as if that was popular knowledge for everyone.

Trisha laughed. "One and the same. But where'd you hear that?"

"Jake." Nicole giggled.

"If you ask me, I think he's sweet on her," Trisha countered with a mischievous grin. "She's new in town too. Came here just about the time you did."

"That's really nice of her, though, to continue traditions in a place she hasn't been to for so long," Nicole said. "I vaguely remember her. It's been so long."

"Today, you can catch up and also help me with these cookies," Trisha said. "You're not just going to eat them all."

Nicole snickered playfully. "Last time I joined you in something, I ended up with a hangover."

Trisha laughed. "I promise, there's no bourbon in these."

"Okay then." Nicole returned. But what else was she going to do? "I just need this headache to wear off first, and then I'll dive in."

"Go lay on the couch. It shouldn't be much longer now. And drink some more of that water," her mother demanded.

"Yes, ma'am," she quipped, saluting her before she walked gingerly to the couch.

It was a good fifteen minutes later before she was able to walk normally again. The pounding had stopped, and she returned upstairs to wash up and change.

When she returned downstairs, her mother was starting a fresh batter. "You want to get the mixer, honey?"

"Sure," Nicole replied. "What are we making this time?"

"Princess-themed cookies." Trisha grinned.

"That sounds interesting," Nicole said.

"I've got the frosting for the clothes, and the sprinkles, and color for the hair and clothes. I'm going to need the piping bags too."

"This is a whole production you're making, huh?" Nicole asked, laughing.

"You have no idea what these people come up with. Simple oatmeal, raisin, and chocolate chip cookies aren't cutting it anymore. I want to win!" she affirmed deviously.

Nicole giggled. "Okay, then. Competitive much?"

"Very," Trisha told her. "Now, pass me the flour."

They busied themselves making vanilla cookies that were slowly transformed into characters from *Frozen, Sleeping Beauty, and The Little Mermaid.* Even Nicole was impressed when they were splayed out on the counter.

"Are people going to eat these?" Nicole wanted to know as she looked on.

"Maybe. The kids might," Trisha replied with a shrug. "Doesn't matter to me one way or another. As long as I win."

"And speaking of winning. I've been thinking, Mom. The shop is a lot to handle. I mean, I've only been here for two weeks, and the number of things in there is overwhelming." She was hoping she'd convince her to eventually sell it. "Are you sure you're going to be able to manage it on your own?"

Trisha sighed and sat on the stool with her shoulders slumped. "I don't think so."

Nicole really didn't expect that the fight would have been that easy. She expected her mother to put up a fight. "Really?"

"Yeah," she admitted, then looked over at her. "I mean, I started it after you and your father left just so I could have something to occupy my time. But it's not making a heap of money, and it's getting harder to keep track of things. That's why I called you down here."

"Mom," Nicole murmured sadly, feeling somewhat ashamed of her original intentions. "I'm sorry. I wish it didn't have to be like this."

"I'm not getting any younger, honey." She turned to Nicole and smiled. "It was bound to happen one day."

"Yeah, but not yet." Nicole exhaled loudly. She felt as if she was already changing her mind about selling it altogether. Especially after hearing about the history of the town and how unique it was. It could be great again, and the antique shop would be an integral part of that. After all, it was the only one in town of its kind.

Alan sure didn't look as if he was interested in selling antiques. He had other plans for that piece of property.

"Did I tell you about that developer?" Nicole finally asked.

"Yes, he's been sniffing around. Came by a few times," Trisha replied, scrunching up her face.

"I don't trust him," Nicole admitted. "And neither does Jake."

"Neither does anybody!" Trisha told her. "He seems like he is intent on buying all the shops and leveling the town. No sirree!"

"I agree. This town has its charms. It just needs a little fixing up in some places, but it's not that bad. In fact, I think I could live here."

"Really?" Trisha's face lit up.

"Don't get any ideas, Mom. I said I think." Nicole laughed.

Trisha clicked her teeth. "Why are you teasing me?"

"I have a life back in Seattle," Nicole replied, letting out a sigh.

"Uh-oh," Trisha said. "I recognize that sound. What's wrong?"

Nicole had never really talked about what her life was like after Rudy. She had a job that she didn't even love, *and* she hated who she worked with. It was beginning to feel like a pebble in her shoe.

"Nothing," she responded as she played with her fingers. "It's just that I don't love my job anymore, and my boss is a pain in the you know what. Lately, I've just felt like a hamster on a wheel...it's turning, but I'm not going anywhere."

"Oh, honey," Trisha exclaimed. "I thought everything was going well. You didn't come home, so I thought things were going so well that I had to pry you away from there."

"I wish." Nicole sighed again, then wiped her hand down her face. "Since Rudy, and then when Stevie left...I don't know. I've just been going through the motions."

"But you talk about your patients all the time," Trisha said as her face contorted in confusion.

"I know. I love that part. Helping people. But the work itself— not so great."

"So, why don't you just go somewhere else?"

"I've tried. Not many places need X-ray technicians, and I got tired of the rejects. I was even contemplating switching careers, but who am I kidding? At forty-three, that would be like pushing water uphill."

"It's never too late, I always say." Her mother smiled. "But I'm sorry to hear that."

"Yeah, that's another reason why I came. I just needed a change of scenery to clear my head. Maybe I'll go back to that. I don't know. I walked out, but I sort of left the bridge intact."

"That's good," Trisha replied. "At least you'll have a backup just in case whatever you're planning doesn't work out."

"Yeah." She sighed again and smeared the countertop with her doodling as she spoke.

"I know what will cheer you up," Trisha said as she hopped off the stool and grabbed Nicole's arm.

"What?" Nicole asked as she tagged along.

"A holiday movie," Trisha said excitedly. "And maybe we could start decorating the tree."

"Ugh. Just shoot me now," Nicole wailed when they got to the sofa. "Mom, I don't like Christmas movies. And please don't tell me it's *Miracle on 34th Street*. And decorating the tree? That's even worse."

Trisha laughed. "There are a whole lot more than that. As for the tree, you don't want me to do that all by myself, do you?"

"I don't want you to do it at all. There's enough lights in Yuletide Creek to light up this house too."

Trisha chuckled. "I don't care what you say. I'm getting a tree this afternoon from Rooney's. Then you and I are going to decorate it. And that's final."

"I hate it when you get so bossy," Nicole whined playfully, like a child, which only amused Trisha.

"But first, it's Christmas movies. Let me get the cocoa and biscuits and make this a jolly morning."

Nicole sat on the sofa. "I can't believe I'm doing this. Both Jake and Stevie would laugh to pieces if they saw me right now."

Trisha laughed. "I bet they would," she quipped as she returned with the biscuits. "Cocoa will be ready in a few, but we'll find a movie by then.

"Obviously, you're the one who'll be searching. I don't even know what to look for," Nicole said in defeat, hoping her bad mood would deter her mother.

It didn't even remotely work.

"Here we go," Trisha announced gleefully. "*Christmas with the Cranks!*"

"Sounds just as fun," Nicole replied sarcastically. "I think I'll enjoy the cocoa and biscuits more."

Trisha snickered. "Such a Debbie Downer. And you used to love Christmas so much."

"Yeah, that was a long time ago. A lot has happened since then."

"Oh, honey." Trisha breathed out, cradling her. "I'm so sorry you had to go through so much. But we can't have all your other Christmases ruined. Besides, if there's any time of year that can cheer you up, it's this one. So, what do you say? We make some new and better memories?" she asked, then wagged her brows. "We can even invite Jake over."

"Mom." Nicole chuckled. "Are you seriously playing cupid right now?"

"Why not? Jake's a fine young man. He's attractive and single..."

"I think I hear the kettle," Nicole interrupted her.

Trisha shook her head and got up. "You're missing out."

"Let's just watch the movie," Nicole told her when she returned.

"Oh, now you want to watch the movie," Trisha attested, rolling her eyes.

"Yes. Better that than listening to my mother playing cupid."

"Fine," Trisha replied, passing her the cup.

Nicole placed it to her lips, but it was already too late. Her mother had already pushed Jake further into her mind.

It was going to be hard to extract him now that she had her blessing.

And she wasn't sure she wanted to try.

Chapter Nine

"Time to go," Trisha said excitedly as she collected her trays of wrapped cookies.

"If these don't win, I'm never helping you with another production," Nicole whined as she grabbed a tray.

"Oh, look, it's snowing," Trisha pointed out when they got to the porch.

"I hope it's being kept indoors," Nicole said as they hurried to the car.

"Doubt it," Trisha returned, setting the cookies gently on the back seat. "It's usually outdoors."

"So not so fun this year," Nicole complained and got into the car.

"Not really," Trisha replied as she got in too. "It's not really snowing that hard. Who knows? It might clear up by evening. Long enough for me to win." She chuckled.

Nicole did too. "Since when did you get this competitive?"

"I don't know. It's a cookie thing. I love baking, and I

want to be better. But then, there's Yvette Alderman," she scoffed.

"Let me guess," Nicole said as she backed out of the driveway. "The competition."

"Did you know she wanted her house to be the Christmas House when Ruth died? I was so glad when Ally showed up and took it over."

"What was so wrong about that?" Nicole asked. "Who said the Christmas House had to be the same house? They should rotate it."

"It's tradition," she explained. "And it's not even about the house. Ruth started this whole thing, and every year people looked forward to all the things she did— the cookie contest, the toy drive, the caroling, the gingerbread house competition— now that's something you should see." She smiled. "Yvette Alderman doesn't have an ounce of Christmas spirit. She just sits up there on her hill like the queen bee."

"Okay, then," Nicole replied. "Guess there's no love lost there."

"Nope. And I'm not the only one who thinks so," Trisha said emphatically.

"I hear you," Nicole said as the car turned onto the street where the Christmas House sat. And there wasn't a doubt in Nicole's mind as to why it was dubbed the Christmas House. Only Santa Claus's shop at the North Pole would beat it. "This is beautiful."

"Told ya." Trisha grinned.

Nicole couldn't take her eyes off the house. It had lights running up and down on the roof where a large Sleigh held a jolly, waving Santa Claus. Candy canes and nutcracker guards were posted by the walkway, with lights illuminating a path to the wraparound porch. One large tree rested on the right side of the lawn, covered in lights, red bows, tinsel, ribbons, and bells. Surrounding it were reindeer that appeared to be chasing each other to the back of the yard, and multicolored lights framed the fencing all around.

"This is insane," Nicole gushed. "It must have taken forever to decorate.

"Hi, welcome." A young woman approached them and held her hand out.

"Oh, thanks," Nicole told her. "I'm Nicole, and this is my mother, Trisha."

"Nice to meet you. I'm Marnie." She smiled beneath the red and green Christmas-themed hat she wore.

"Where do we put these?" Trisha asked.

"Wow, those look great. There's a spot under that tent." She pointed.

"Thank you, dear," Trisha replied as they walked off to the tent that was fully white but was laced with green and red scarves and trimmed with stockings and other Christmas accessories.

"All right, let's get one thing straight," Nicole said after they'd placed their cookies on the table. "We are never going to have the Christmas House. I could barely decorate one tree. And look at this? How long did this take?"

"I'm guessing days," Trisha told her. "But wait until you see the inside."

"I can imagine," Nicole said. And she was just as blown away after the tour. A fully loaded Christmas tree was in almost every room. Garlands ran down the banisters that led upstairs, and white lights wrapped around them. Christmas favorites streamed through hidden speakers, and the house smelled like pine, cinnamon, and spices.

"Okay, it's official," Nicole declared, then turned around. "Where is this Ally person?"

Trisha laughed and pointed. Nicole walked over and tapped her on the shoulder. "Hi."

Ally's face lit up. "Hello, there."

"You're Ally?" Nicole asked to be sure just so she could rightly place the compliment.

The woman nodded in acknowledgment.

"Wonderful. I'm Nicole, and that's my mother, Trisha. She runs the antique shop," she explained by way of introduction. "And this house is crazy."

"I know, right?" Ally laughed. "I got a little carried away."

"I must admit, I wasn't all that into Christmas, but you should know you're turning me around," she said.

"That's amazing news. Well, I'm glad you think so. The children love it too."

"I bet they do," Nicole replied. "But don't let us keep you. I know you have other guests wanting to compliment you."

Ally smiled and nodded as Nicole and Trisha walked off and picked up two cups of hot cocoa from the station on the porch.

"I don't think the snow's easing up, Mom," Nicole said as she observed the flurries turning into huge fluffy snowflakes.

"Hmm," she mused. "I really hope this is the worst it gets. All of the cookies are outside," she lamented. "It would be a shame if they got ruined."

"Well, let's be hopeful it doesn't get worse," Nicole replied. "Let's see what's happening over there." She motioned to a group of people who were gathered around some children.

It turned out they were just goofing around, and it wasn't a part of the planned event.

"Can you believe him? He came into my store, asking if I wanted to sell," a woman huffed behind them. "The nerve."

"He's been busy. I don't trust him," another woman said.

"You shouldn't," a man grunted. "I've had that bakery for years. It's been in my family for four generations. I'm not selling it to some young blood who just wants to tear it down. Next thing you know, they'll put us out. We can't even afford to live in the properties they put up."

"Or afford anything," the first woman added.

It was hard for Nicole not to listen in. She knew they were talking about Alan, but she could see no one liked him. Maybe the town was just full of discerners who could spot a fake a mile away.

"What about you, Trisha?" someone asked, pulling her mother into the conversation. "Has he come to you?"

"He has. And my daughter too," Trisha replied with annoyance. "He caught her in the diner of all places."

"And everywhere else," Nicole joined in. "I didn't think anything of it at first until he just started showing up everywhere."

"He did the same thing to me," the woman who'd spoken first said. Nicole recognized her as the woman who operated the florist shop. She looked deeply concerned. "What if we don't have a choice?"

"What do you mean, don't have a choice?" the

gentleman boomed. "They're not buying me out, that's for sure."

"You know how sometimes they go into small towns, these big moguls, and bully the townspeople into submission," the first woman said again and crossed her arms over her chest. "Remember what they did to the Native Americans? It could happen to us. They could just force us out."

"Nobody's forcing us out of anything," Nicole fired back. "If he could do that, he wouldn't be walking around asking everybody. They can't just bulldoze the properties either."

"That's right," another woman replied. "And I'm not selling."

There was a chorus of "me neither."

"I mean, Yuletide Creek is a special place. It's not like any other town," Trisha said while the others nodded in agreement. "The thing about this place is its uniqueness, you know? You never know what you'll get when you come into town, and that's not something you can get just about anywhere."

"That's right," the gentleman agreed. "We need to stick together so no one pushes us out. We have to stand together!" he repeated for emphasis, though his bushy brows dipped slightly to reveal he was also a little worried.

But the talk of special and unique sent Nicole's mind to the jewelry box she'd found. It was a part of the store's inventory, so by right, she couldn't just take it. So, she thought about asking her mother for it because, as Jake had said, it's a dime a dozen and just junk.

But the thought of keeping it made her guilty as well. She'd always chastised her mother for holding on to every shiny thing she ever laid her eyes on, and there she was about to do the same thing. She decided to hold off on that thought. Maybe she'd change her mind and put the box back on the shelf.

"The wind is really picking up," Trisha stated as she rubbed her palms together. "I thought for sure it would have let up by now."

"This isn't good," the man gestured to the tents. The scarves were already flapping in the wind, and one of them had come loose. "The thing looks like it's about to give way."

"Oh, dear!" Trisha exclaimed. "Maybe we should take this inside."

"Too many people," the florist responded. "It has to be outside."

"Someone should have told that to Mother Nature," the florist replied. "Look! Some people are starting to leave."

"It's not that bad," Trisha said defensively, and Nicole smiled to herself. She knew her mother was more concerned about winning the contest than whether they got snowed in or not.

"Yes, it is, Mom," Nicole told her. "We should probably get going."

"Help!" someone cried, and all eyes found the tent, the one that housed the cookies for the contest. Trisha hurried over just in time to see some of the items sliding off the table.

"This wind is getting too strong," Owen, the town grocer, cried as he rushed to the back of the tent and tried to keep it upright. "This thing is going to cave."

"I think we should just take our cookies and go,"

another competitor said right before she darted inside and took her tray.

Nicole watched in horror as Marnie and Owen struggled to keep the tent together. "I think this side is pinned down!" Owen shouted over the whistling wind.

"Mom, that's our cue," Nicole told Trisha. "Get the cookies. This one is done for."

She saw the look on her mother's face and where she was looking. She turned, and the woman in white wearing the red lipstick and a smirk told her that it must be Yvette Alderman. Her mother had been right. She looked too pleased with something that was so well put together that was now ruined.

"I bet she had something to do with it," Trisha declared grudgingly as she grabbed her trays and handed one to Nicole.

"I doubt she had anything to do with the wind and snow." Nicole giggled at her mother's silliness.

"Not that. The tent," Trisha replied, pointing.

She'd barely said the words when there was a squeal, and the tent came crashing down. Nicole's heart melted when she saw Ally standing in the middle of the yard with a look of dismay.

Yvette Alderman walked by them just then. "Well, that ends that event. What a shame." She smirked, then started humming as she headed to her car.

"You know, Mom," Nicole said as they raced to get inside their car too. "I think you may be onto something with that woman. She is as mean as the Grinch himself."

"Told you," Trisha replied, for what felt like the hundredth time that day. "She is rotten to the core. I bet she's glad it's ruined. Did you see her shortbread? It was a shame— damned thing was burned. She wouldn't even have come last."

Nicole laughed. "Doesn't matter now," she said as they pulled off the curb. "We'll never know now."

And as she left, she spotted Ally, still standing motionless, as the wind whipped her scarf around her neck.

Chapter Ten

"Mom!" Nicole called from the bathroom.

She brushed the light foundation on her face and turned about in the mirror, surveying her look. She was happy about one thing—jeans and a sweatshirt. That was all she needed to wear to the store every day. Not scrubs. Not mules. Not Crocs. Just whatever she wanted, and she loved the freedom of it. She pulled her hair back at her nape and brushed the sides before she realized she hadn't heard her mother.

"Mom?" she called again as she exited the bathroom. Still, no response. Nicole's heart started to race as she darted to her mother's room. "Mom? Where are you?"

"In here," she called from her bathroom. "I came in here, sat down, and then couldn't move again."

"What happened?" Nicole asked as she helped her mother up and got her dressed.

"I don't know. Ah!" she cried out, clutching her lower back. "Damn thing has been acting up again."

Nicole narrowed her eyes. "Mom, why didn't you tell me? What if you'd hurt yourself?"

"I'm fine." She waved her off. "Just give me a couple of minutes, and I'll be fine."

"Just a few seconds ago, you couldn't even get off the toilet, and now you want to stand all day at the store. Not happening," Nicole said firmly. "Today is your unofficial day off."

"But..."

"No buts. You're going to either lay in bed and read a book or sit by the fire and watch a movie. Dealer's choice."

Trisha sulked. "Fine. But that means you're in charge today."

"I'm pretty sure I can handle it," Nicole told her. "I'll see you later, and please don't do any heavy lifting or bending. Which means you don't get to start working on that Christmas tree. Stevie and I will do it when she gets here. Two weeks of that thing should be more than enough. So, just relax."

"Of course." Trisha smiled.

"Okay, see you later." Nicole blew her mom a kiss, then walked out.

It wasn't until she was at the store and about to step inside that she realized she was going to be alone with Jake. All day. At least she wouldn't have her mother's interfering and annoying winks and nods, but that only meant they'd have more time— maybe too much time alone.

She sucked in her breath and walked in nervously. Her heart was racing, and her gaze darted around the room, looking for any signs of him.

"Morning!"

"Jeez!" Nicole jumped, then clamped her hand over her chest right before she slapped Jake on the arm. "Don't do that."

"Ow!" he cried playfully.

She rolled her eyes at him. "You're lucky I didn't kick you in the gonads."

"Ouch!" he pretended to wince, then pulled his legs together, much to her amusement. "You're a very violent woman," he snickered, wagging his finger at her.

"Only when provoked. Now you've been warned. I will not be held responsible for what I do when someone sneaks up on me."

Jake chuckled and saluted her. "Aye, aye, Capt'n!"

She giggled. "You're so silly."

"Where's Mrs. Hayes?" he asked, peering outside.

"Oh, no, she isn't here. Out with a bad back."

"That again?" he asked with concern. "How's she doing?"

"Let's just say she sat down and couldn't get back up, and then she wanted to come in," Nicole reported while she headed for the small office with Jake in tow. "I had to put her on bed rest. Luckily, I'm here."

"I could have handled it," Jake told her as he leaned against the door jam. "It's not the first time it's flared up."

"That's not very comforting." Nicole sighed, rubbing her forehead.

"What? That I was running the store all by myself?" he asked, wrinkling his brows.

She started to laugh. "No. That her back keeps acting up. How did she ever plan on running this store for much longer? I mean, there's always a reason to bend over, or pick something up, or reach up high, or climb a ladder."

She sank into the chair. "Hey, Mrs. Hayes is a tough woman."

"Who's at home right now with a back problem." Nicole sighed again. "I think we should probably get started. With her gone, I need to make a serious dent in getting things sorted and throwing out what we don't need, and I'm pretty sure there are plenty."

"Okay, let's go," he called her with his hand as he walked off.

"What, you don't have a new display theme to arrange?" she teased.

He chuckled. "Don't tempt me."

They walked in silence, but it was hard for her not to pay attention to his broad shoulders and the way his body narrowed at his waist. She could imagine the muscles underneath rippling like water disturbed on a lake.

"So," he started to say, then stopped abruptly, and she crashed right into him.

"Sorry." She blushed and looked away.

"Are you okay?" he asked, then started to laugh again.

"Yes, I'm fine," she retorted.

"Hold on. I think you've got something in your..." He didn't finish the statement. He just reached over and brushed something lightly off the side of her head. "There," he said with a smile that penetrated her soul and melted other parts of her.

"Thanks," she replied, even though she wasn't sure if he'd picked anything off her in the first place. Maybe he just wanted to touch her, and the thought of that made her smile.

"I was about to say we can start here. I'll get some of the heavy stuff out of the way, and you can start tagging the smaller ones," he suggested.

"Works for me," Nicole said.

She started tagging items and tossing some in a box she kept nearby for broken items. Or just weird ones that didn't seem to have any purpose and that may have been around at the time of the dinosaurs.

"Hey, not that!" Jake called out, then practically hurled himself at her, grabbing a China doll from her grip. "This is a classic."

She rolled her eyes. "Let me guess. It once belonged to a Mongolian princess."

He laughed so hard he had to lean against the shelf to his right. "You're so irreverent. But no, not a Mongolian princess. It's a part of a collection. The other pieces are around here somewhere. I'll hold on to it."

She shook her head and resumed her tagging. That wasn't the last time that Jake saved an item she was about to toss— one was a French cuisine cookbook that was written in French. No one in town spoke French. Then there was the three-legged stool, or should she have said, the two-and-a-half-legged stool— he was confident he could fix it up and sell it. And yes, there was also the giant enamel teapot that George Washington probably used to make tea.

"You're tiring," she finally said to him. "I'm beginning to think you're worse than Mom."

He laughed. "You just have no appreciation for the fine arts."

She snickered. "Fine art? Yeah, that's what it is. I lack appreciation."

He chuckled softly, but even with his antics, Nicole found that she enjoyed his company a great deal. He made her feel warm and mushy on the inside, and she dreaded the day coming to an end.

"We can do this part now," Jake said as he pointed to a large bookcase-looking item in the righthand corner of the store.

"Ugh!" Nicole groaned, throwing her hands in the air. "Might as well."

"I'll pull it away from the wall so you can get to it better," he told her. There were some smaller items in front of it, and he wormed his way around several items to try and find a decent fit to squeeze the smaller items through.

It was tiring watching him move one item after another and trying to find space to fit them all. At last, he was able to move the bench that was before the bookcase, but when he did, it revealed a trapdoor in the floor.

"Whoa! What's that?" Nicole asked, pointing at the floor.

"Hmm," Jake grunted, then leaned over to inspect further. "It looks like some door or the other. Probably an old root cellar."

"Can you open it?" she asked excitedly.

He turned to look at her from his bent-over position. "Are you serious?"

"Yes!" she replied, moving closer. "What if there's buried treasure down there."

Jake shook his head and then tried to pull on the latch. "It's swollen shut, but it's just as well." He stood, dusting off his hands on his jeans.

"Aren't you curious about what's down there?" she asked him as she stared at the door still.

"No, I'm not curious. This place has been here for over a hundred years. Whatever's down there would be long dead."

"Not if it's a treasure," she shot mischievously.

Jake looked at her as if she was simple-minded. "Treasure? Really?"

"Why not? People bury stuff all the time, and then

they die, and no one knows about it," she said with all the childlike excitement she could muster.

"Okay, first of all, that only happens in the movies. Real people don't bury their valuables in an underground basement. They have vaults for things like that. Besides, when the property was inspected, don't you think they would have found anything that was down there?"

"Not really?" She grinned. "But you know what? I'm going to find out. That's my reward for all this labor. A fat treasure, and I'm not sharing it with you."

He laughed. "If nothing else, it's good to see you excited for once, but I wish you would have told me."

"Told you what?" She wrinkled her brows.

"That if I had dressed up like a pirate and shown up with a treasure map, I'd have gotten your attention sooner."

Nicole blushed. "You got it soon enough without it," she said, then cleared her throat. She couldn't believe she'd just said that, but the look on his face told her he had approved.

All parts of her were singing and whistling at that point, and she could feel the sweat beads forming in droves. If she didn't move from that spot, there was no telling what she might do. And the look in his eyes told her he wouldn't stop her.

"Is that right?" he asked, moving closer to her.

Oh, no!

Her heart hammered as he stood right before her, and when he lifted his hand to smooth a stray lock of her hair back behind her ear, she shivered, and her eyes closed involuntarily. She felt as if her skin was burning, and she could already feel his lips on hers.

But he didn't.

"You know, I saw you that first day you came in, and I was like, wow." He smiled. "But I came to realize that you were a little guarded. I mean, I recognize it because I'm the same way. It's what happens when you've been burned before."

"Yeah?" she asked, then gulped. "You're not wrong."

He sighed and pulled up a stool for her while he leaned against the bookshelf. "I was in love before. Proposed to her. Almost made it to the altar too. But she didn't show. I haven't seen her since," he admitted as a nostalgic look flooded his eyes. "I'm not even sure what happened. Maybe I wasn't good enough. Maybe she wanted something I couldn't give. But I'd invested everything I had into that relationship for four years. And then she took off. I don't know," he pondered, then wiped his hand down his face. "That's not something you get over easily."

"I know what you mean. I was married to a grunge musician. Had groupies all over the place. I was one of them, in a sense. Or the girl he took everywhere until I got pregnant and lost my mobility. I was easily replaced several times over until he just stopped coming home. So, now it's just Stevie and me."

"Wow," he replied, then slapped his leg. "We make quite the pair, huh?"

"Tell me about it." She grinned sadly. "Makes it hard to trust again."

"Yep," he agreed, then gazed into her eyes. "Something tells me I can take a chance with you, though."

The butterflies in her stomach started fluttering, and her heart felt as if it would leap right through her chest. "I feel the same way. And so does my mother."

He laughed. "Is that so?"

"Yeah. She's been singing your praises."

"All right, all right. Thank you, Mrs. Hayes." He chuckled. "Tell you what? How about we just keep things nice and simple?"

"Things?" she asked nervously.

"Yes. Us. Whatever this is, and I know it's something. Let's start off slow and see what happens."

She smiled. Nicole was sure her face resembled the Christmas House. "I'd like that."

"Ditto!" He grinned. "How about dinner? We're the bosses today. We can lock up early."

"Sounds like a plan," Nicole agreed. Her head was spinning after that. It had been a while since she'd been on the dating scene, but she was super excited about it, even though she wasn't sure what it meant— it had been so long, but the all-work-no-play days for her had to come to an end.

The day couldn't end fast enough!

Chapter Eleven

Luckily for them, it wasn't a busy day at all.

Not many people came in, and because the display case hadn't changed much, it didn't spark as much awe and wonder. This also meant Nicole was able to make a dent in her job after all— she got much of the left side of the shop cleaned out and organized, which left mainly the front.

She wasn't sure why she was even organizing the shop still when they just might have an everything-must-go sale soon, considering that her mother may not be able to maintain the store for much longer.

Her gaze kept finding the clock as the hours seemed to drag on, and the closer they got to closing time, the more anxious she became.

Until she noticed Jake washing up and that the clock read eight.

"Ready?" he asked.

"Ugh, yeah, I think so," she said, looking around. "I think the shop will survive without us."

He laughed and held the door open so she could pass. "Let's go then."

Once Nicole was out the door, he turned out the lights and joined her on the sidewalk. She hadn't noticed before, but Jake drove a black Toyota Tacoma truck. He opened the door for her, and she climbed in, fully conscious of how close he was to her and of his hand brushing against hers, igniting every dead cell in her body.

She sucked in a deep breath as he hurried to the driver's seat and started the truck.

"So, where are we going?" Nicole asked as he turned onto Main Street.

"Are you into seafood?" he glanced across the seat, asking.

"Uh, not my favorite unless it's really good," she replied. "Is that what you had in mind?"

Oh, I know where we'll go. There's this place called The Smorgasbord about a mile from here."

"What do they have?" Nicole asked curiously. She'd always been very picky with her choice of food, and she didn't think Yuletide Creek would have what she liked for date night.

Date night. Who would have thought I'd ever have another one?

"That's an interesting name. What do they serve, or should I assume from the name?" She smiled.

"You can assume, and you'd be right. They serve from apples to alligators in that place. Whatever you want, they've got it." He grinned. Then he looked across at her as they rolled up to a traffic light. "Just don't order alligator."

She giggled. "I promise I won't. Can't make any promises if they serve bats, though."

He wrinkled his face. "Eww! You're worse than I thought."

She laughed so airily she surprised herself. She'd found herself laughing mostly on the outside or when she was expected to. And she'd learned to smile when she was paid to do it on her job. But with Jake, the laugh was real, and it resonated inside her, warming her from head to toe.

"I sincerely doubt that," she responded and relaxed in her seat, leaning her head against the headrest as she looked out the window. She felt nineteen all over again.

The Smorgasbord was more popular than she thought it was. "Wow. It seems everyone is here."

"Believe it or not, most of these folks are from out of town. They just came for the Christmas events," he said, then pulled into a parking spot.

"Are you serious? This many people? Wow!"

"Yep." He nodded. "The town's not so dead after all."

"I'm blown away. Maybe because I'm stuck in the store all the time, I don't really notice what's going on around me."

"Someone should change that," Jake said, winking at her.

And she wished she could just stop blushing so much. If she was guaranteed a certain amount of blush at birth, she'd have milked it since she met Jake.

They got out and were met at the door by a hostess who showed them to an intimate seating area for two. There was soft lighting in the establishment, perpetuated by plated lights that gave off a romantic vibe. Their table was already dressed with a food and drink menu that was placed on rustic tables. There were golden runners on each table and a floral centerpiece for a nice touch.

"This is nice," Nicole commented as she looked around. "Doesn't sound like the name."

He laughed. "What did you expect? People sitting around rocks and eating with their hands?"

She giggled. "Now that you mention it."

"Come on," he groaned. "You can do better than that."

"Okay, fine. I'll behave," she said, picking up the food menu. He reached for the drinks. She hid the smile behind the rectangular, laminated menu and searched it for something spectacular. "You weren't kidding. They have all sorts of things from everywhere— Asian, Caribbean, American, Spanish, English...how many cooks do they have?"

"They try to cater to everyone, which is why this is a great spot. Something for everyone. Oh, wait, I think I want to surprise you with one of my favorites."

"Ooh, will I like it?" she asked excitedly. "I'm a little scared."

He chuckled. "You definitely will," he replied. "Excuse me." He slid out of his chair. He met the waiter before he got to the table and ordered his secret meal.

Nicole's butterflies started acting up again. She couldn't remember the last time she felt that excited. She couldn't wait to see what he'd ordered for her. He was wearing a broad grin when he returned and wouldn't budge even though she pestered him for an answer.

"You'll just have to wait and see," he told her. "Don't you like surprises?"

"No. Yes. Not with food. What if I'm allergic? Or I hate it?" she asked nervously.

"Hmm," he mused. "You have a point, but telling you won't make a difference. If you are allergic, then we'll get something else. If not, you're going to try something new tonight."

She pouted. "You're bossy."

He chuckled, placing his forearms on the table as he leaned forward and stared at her, causing another of her infamous blushes. "You blush easily," he told her, which didn't help. "I like it. Makes you even more beautiful."

Nicole wanted him to shut up. Or kiss her. Or something else. Anything else other than just sitting there driving her insane. "Thank you," she told him. "You make blushing too easy," she replied, then looked away. "You're making me feel like a young woman again."

"You deserve to feel that way," he said softly. "I'm sorry you were ever hurt."

She glanced up at him and their eyes locked. She couldn't remember if anyone had ever told her that. "Thank you. Really," she said to him, then looked down to keep her tears away.

He noticed and dialed it back. He didn't want to ruin the mood by making her think about her ex-husband. The relief was real when the waiter approached with the meal.

When he set it down on the table, Nicole almost keeled over. "Caribbean," she burst instantly. "I recognize the flavor. What is this?" she asked either the waiter or Jake, anyone who cared to answer.

The waiter responded. "Jerked chicken served with rice and peas, fried ripe plantains, festival, and steamed Bok choy." She looked across and saw Jake had ordered the same for himself.

"Any allergies?" he asked.

"None," she replied as her mouth watered.

"Enjoy your meal," the waiter said. "I'll be back in a few minutes with your drink." He then walked off.

Nicole didn't hesitate. "I tasted this once, a long time ago, but I couldn't find a decent place again," she said in between bites as she savored the juicy, spicy meat that slid from the bone. "Thank you, Jake."

He grinned with all the pride in Yuletide Creek. "You're welcome. I'm glad you like it."

"I should let you order for me from now on," she said, suggesting there would be more dates.

He wore a grin from ear to ear. "You can count on that."

They spent the rest of the evening laughing and talking about this and that, everything and nothing. At the end of it, Nicole knew he'd won her over. He was charming and not forceful at all.

"This evening was really nice," Nicole said as they got to the truck. "I really needed this."

"I know, I could tell." He winked, then stared into her eyes as he leaned closer.

Her heart raced as she realized what was about to happen. He was leaning in closer, and she could almost taste his lips when she jumped.

"Oh my gosh," she burst when her phone vibrated against her side.

She wondered if it was a coincidence that his also started ringing too. They looked at each other, and both fished out the devices quickly.

"It's Mom," Nicole said.

"Mine too," he replied.

"Mom? What's wrong?" she asked, worried that she'd probably fallen and couldn't get up. Or worse. "Are you okay?"

"I'm fine," Trisha told her. "It's the shop. Someone broke in."

"What?" Nicole asked as her heart started to race for a different reason.

"What?" Jake echoed the same words as his eyes popped.

Nicole's heart raced. "Someone broke into the shop. Have you called the cops? How did you know?"

"Someone who was passing saw and called me. Where are you?" her mother asked.

"I'm not that far at all. I'll head there now." Nicole hung up and hopped into the truck. "Let's go," she told Jake, the kiss now long forgotten.

Her heart thumped hard as they drove. "It's like someone was watching us," Jake said. "It's only nine. This is the time we'd normally close, so they knew no one was there."

"That's creepy," Nicole shuddered. "Who would want to rob an antique store? There's nothing of value in there, and we already cleared out what little money there was in the cash register. This doesn't make any sense."

They saw the red and blue flashing lights as they approached the shop. They parked behind the cruiser and hopped out.

"Hi, I'm Nicole. This is my mother's shop," she told the officer. "What happened?"

"Good evening, ma'am. Jake," the officer greeted, then tipped the front of his hat out of respect.

"Hey, Nick. What's going on? How'd they get in?"

"Looks like they broke the window," he said, his hands firmly placed on his hips. "Can you go in and have a look around to see if anything is missing?"

"That's gonna be hard to do with all the trinkets in that place." Nicole sighed, still confused at the ludicrousness of the act. "But who would do such a thing?"

"Our best bet is out-of-town vandals," Officer Nick replied as he walked in behind them. "Watch your step. There's glass everywhere."

The store was a sight. All of Nicole's hard work was now lying mostly on the ground. "Looks like they were looking for something," she said aloud.

"Like what?" Officer Nick asked as his foot pushed stuff out of the way.

"No clue. Probably won't figure it out tonight, either. I was just trying to organize the items in the store, and I wasn't done yet," she moped.

Nicole couldn't help thinking it was Alan. He'd wanted to buy the shop, but they'd refused to give in to his offers. He must have wanted something inside. But what? She looked around, but nothing was readily identifiable, and she couldn't tell the cops her suspicion because she had no proof.

"Okay, we'll wrap this up and log the evidence we have so far. If you notice anything else, please let us know," Officer Nick said, tipping his hat again, and then walked out.

Nicole leaned against the glass counter, staring at the lights in utter dismay until they all left, and all that remained were the twinkling lights in the stores' display windows.

"What are you thinking?" Jake asked her promptly.

"Maybe nothing, but I think that guy Alan may have something to do with it," she told him.

"You mean that sketchy guy from the restaurant and the tree lighting?" he asked, raising a brow. Nicole nodded yes. "Why would he do that?"

"Because he wants to buy the shop. Maybe he wanted something in here only an owner could get. I don't know."

Jake palmed the back of his neck at this new information. "I'm sorry, what? He wants to buy the shop. How come I never heard about this?"

"I don't know!" she replied. "I thought you knew. He's apparently asking everyone to sell."

"That snake. I knew there was something rotten about him," he snapped.

"Well, I think you were correct."

But she couldn't help thinking if it were Alan, what was he looking for? And did he find it?

Chapter Twelve

All of Nicole's efforts had been wasted.

Her heart sank when both she and her mom returned to the shop the following morning. It seemed the night had masked the true extent of the vagrancy— it looked a whole lot worse from her position inside the main door.

"Now I have to go through and fix these all over again," she groaned. "It took so long the first time."

"I'll help." Trisha sighed.

"Mom, you can barely stand ten minutes, let alone hours. Jake will pitch in, I guess. But that's not the point. I'd just finished doing it, and now I have to do it all over again.

Her shoulders sagged as she walked to the office to put her purse down. "When's the locksmith coming?" Nicole asked her mother.

She didn't hear a response, so she turned, and her heart skipped a beat when she saw Jake filling the doorway. "Hey, how are you holding up?"

"Barely," she said, then rubbed her eyes. "I barely got

any sleep at all. And now, I come in here, and it's like the burglar returned to make sure everything's on the floor." She sat at the edge of the desk and crossed her arms. "It's just so discouraging to do something you literally just finished doing."

He walked over to her and placed his hands on her shoulders, and gently massaged them. "Don't worry too much," he told her. "Just take your time. There's no deadline on this. And you have me." He grinned.

"Yeah." She smiled up at him. "Thanks."

"Hello?" someone called from the front.

Nicole looked up at Jake. He seemed just as curious about the caller.

"Oh, my," a woman said as she covered her mouth. "I heard about the vandalism, but I didn't realize it was this bad. Do you need a hand, dear? I mean, I can help you to set things right. Lord knows this is going to be a lot of work."

Nicole widened her eyes. "Oh, sure," she gushed. "Thank you, but I'm afraid I don't know your name."

"Oh, everyone calls me Miss Lorraine." She smiled.

"Thank you, Miss Lorraine. I really appreciate it. I was just about to tackle all of this glass that needs cleaning. Mr. Rogers should be coming over with the plyboard for the window."

"Well, where's the broom closet? I'll get started," she said as if she owned the place and walked off.

Jake and Nicole shared pleasing smiles. "Didn't I tell you? You'll be fine."

Little did she realize just how fine she would be. As soon as everyone was awake, it seemed, they found the shop. Everyone not only wanted to know what happened, but they were all eager to pitch in.

"The more of us there are, the quicker it will get done." Mayor Luke grinned when he introduced himself. "I sure hope they didn't take anything," he told Nicole.

He didn't seem like the grinch everyone had made him out to be. "I hope not," Nicole replied. "Mom's depressed about it. She can't even leave the office yet."

"Yeah, that's understandable. Oh, maybe she could see the new doc that came into town. He's just outside. Hold on." He dashed outside.

Nicole turned to Jake. "Is this the same Mayor Luke?" she whispered.

Jake nodded and wagged his brows to indicate Luke was returning. "Dr. Weaver, this is Nicole. Her mother owns the store. Maybe you can introduce yourself," he told the man.

Dr. Weaver had salt-and-pepper hair that was slicked back, revealing his square jaw and laugh lines that creased his eyes. He held out big, warm hands that she shook. "Hello," he greeted her. "Show me the way to my patient."

"Oh, don't call her that just yet." Nicole laughed, then introduced her mother to the doctor. It was interesting how quickly she perked up, and Nicole briefly entertained the idea of hooking them up, much the same as she'd done with her and Jake.

Mayor Luke was still around when she returned. "So, what can I help with?" he asked.

"Umm..." Nicole said, looking around. "The small items go on that shelf. Maybe you could help Miss Lorraine with that."

"Sure thing," he replied, walking off.

"This is incredible," she gushed, watching everyone pitch in to help.

"I know, right?" Dr. Weaver said from behind her. She hadn't realized she'd spoken out loud.

"All these people are amazing," she reiterated. "I didn't expect any of this. I came in this morning feeling so down that I had to do this alone. And look at this," she said, choking on the words.

He chuckled. "I take it you're from the city and not used to anything like this."

"You got that right, Doc. Out there, you're on your own."

But she was even more alone because she'd been so determined to be independent, an island, that she'd forgotten what it was like when people were there to help.

"Say, your mother said you're an X-ray technician?" he asked.

"Yes, that I am," she told him.

"I came here a few weeks ago. Started the clinic down by Bay Street, and I can tell you, I don't miss the big-city medicine. The constant running around. No breaks. No time for anything else."

"Hey, I wasn't a doctor, and I know what you mean. I was thinking the same thing a few days ago about how good it feels to wear jeans and a sweatshirt to work. It's a laid-back feeling I haven't had in a long time."

"So, are you here for the holidays, or is this long-term?" he asked. "I could use some help down at the clinic. I've got my hands full of patients already."

"To be honest, I'm not sure what I'm going to do just yet. In a sense, it depends on what's going on with my mom," she replied honestly.

"I understand that. If you do stick around, let me know, okay?" he asked with a broad smile.

"I will. Thank you for the offer."

He patted her shoulder and walked off to join some other men who were trying to clean out the display case.

With the whole town helping, they had almost everything back where it belonged by evening. What wasn't shelved remained in boxes, but at least the store no longer looked vandalized. On the bright side, Nicole had the empty spaces that would be easier to refill than to rearrange.

Slowly everyone trickled out toward evening, and Nicole thanked them profusely. Trisha was with her to usher them out, but she was still down about the whole incident.

"I think I'm going to call it a night," she finally said. "I'll see you at home, sweetie."

"Okay, Mom," Nicole responded sadly.

It wasn't until around six in the evening that the store was quiet again, and it was just her and Jake once more.

"See?" he asked with a grin. "Ask, and you shall receive, although technically you didn't ask, but the universe knew what help was needed."

She rubbed her eyes and yawned. "Sorry," she said. "I'm starting to feel tired too."

"I bet you are," he replied, inching closer to her.

"Jake, can we talk about what happened?" she asked, then looked away.

He backed up instantly and narrowed his eyes. "What about it?"

"Don't you think you were being a little rude?" she asked him.

His eyes popped. "Rude? You thought I was being rude?"

"Yeah, just a little," she told him.

He held his hands out as if he was bracing against

something, and she could see that he was offended. She wasn't sure why he was, though. He didn't know Alan, so she wasn't sure why he'd reacted to him the way he had. She wondered if he was being jealous or if he was just that type of person. She didn't want to dive in deep with someone she didn't really know.

"Okay," he said tentatively. "I guess that's my cue." He clenched his jaw. "I'm sorry. It was a mistake. I crossed the line, and it won't happen again. It's clear I crossed a line you'd marked for me."

Somehow, she got the feeling that they were thinking about different things. "Are you okay?" she asked him.

"Do you need help with anything else?" he asked abruptly, completely throwing her off guard.

"Uh, no," she said, staring at him curiously. "Jake, what's wrong?"

"You just told me, okay. I'll be more careful next time," he said, brushing past her.

She turned, and her mind started to spin. They were definitely talking about different things. He didn't need to keep his distance when the issue was Alan. In any case, he was overreacting, and she wasn't sure what to do.

"Are you good to lock up?" he asked her from the door.

"I'm leaving now," she answered.

"I'll wait," he replied, walking outside, where he stood for the entire time that it took her to pack up her things and lock up the shop.

"Good night," he mumbled, then walked off.

"Good night," she responded softly. She walked to her car, but she could see that he didn't move until she'd left. At least he was a gentleman still, but she needed to find out what she'd said that made him into a grouch again.

Chapter Thirteen

"Mom, are you going to the shop today?" Nicole asked as she stood by the dining table.

Trisha was drinking her tea and munching on crackers. "No," she replied softly.

"Mom, it's been three days. Don't you plan on ever going back?" she asked. It was clear that she was traumatized by the break-in.

"I don't know." She sighed. "It's just so depressing not even being able to have a display window. It's Christmas, and the store feels so lifeless with that plyboard blocking everything from view. People walking past won't even realize we're open," she moped.

Nicole completely understood her sentiments. "I know, Mom, but you can't just not go back. We're going to get the glass back in no time, and things will go back to the way it was."

"Yeah? And who's gonna pay for that glass?" she asked.

"Well, Mr. Rogers said we could pay him in installments," Nicole said cheerily in hopes of lightening the mood. "And some of the community members have even offered their help again."

"I don't like charity," Trisha returned proudly.

Nicole laughed. "Now you sound like me. I forgot what it feels like to be surrounded by people who care. Not until they all showed up to help with cleaning up the store. It's not charity, Mom. It's compassion."

She huffed shortly before her face lit up. "You know what I want to do? Get away."

Nicole narrowed her eyes. "Get away from what? You're not doing anything."

"From here and now and all of this," she explained, flailing her arms around. "And I have just the thing."

Nicole's brows furrowed. "I do not find that to be a coincidence. You've been planning this, haven't you?"

"Not really," Trisha said, toying with her cup. "It's just that a group of people from town are going to Leaven-worth. I haven't done anything in a while, and this seems like the perfect time to go somewhere. I could get my mind off the shop, and you're here."

Nicole easily understood her mother's depression. She'd lost her Christmas spirit, what with the vandalism and the plyboard making it impossible to have any of her displays. It had taken the fight right out of her, and Nicole was afraid that, if left alone, she'd only get worse.

"Who's gonna handle the shop?" Nicole asked.

"Jake," Trisha replied matter-of-factly. "It's not something he's never done before."

Nicole remembered the conversation she'd had with Jake a couple of days before and how the tension hadn't gotten any better. Maybe she needed the break as much as her mother.

"Okay, fine. I'll go with you," she finally agreed.

"Thank you," Trisha said, then instantly sprang from the chair.

"What's in Leavenworth, by the way?" Nicole asked, heading for the kitchen.

"They're a small town like Yuletide Creek. It's like the North Pole exploded there. You'll love it. And they have all kinds of sights and scenes. We can go shopping."

"Oh, shopping." Nicole grinned. "I can do that."

Trisha laughed. "Some things never change."

"Nope," Nicole beamed. "When do we leave?"

"In two hours," Trisha replied.

"What?" Nicole asked in shock. "Two hours? And you're only now telling me?"

"What? I hadn't made up my mind about it." Trisha shrugged. "Besides, the bus will be on Main Street. Do you really need more than two hours to get ready?"

"Yes!" Nicole exclaimed, then hurried off. "I need to find something to wear," she said as she bounded up the steps like a teenager. "Wait," she said from the top of the stairs. "Will we be staying overnight?"

"Yes," Trisha told her, blushing. "Forgot that tidbit."

Nicole shook her head and walked off. But considering she didn't have her entire wardrobe, choosing an outfit and packing an overnight bag didn't take as long as she thought it would. She was ready in ninety minutes. Trisha was not.

"Wow. After all that talk, I thought you'd be the one annoying the bus driver," Nicole told her mother when she saw her scurrying around her room for things to put into her overnight bag.

"I'm old. I move slower," she replied.

"Excuses, excuses," Nicole said and clicked her teeth.

"Go away!" Trisha playfully tossed a scarf at her. Nicole dodged it, laughed, and then proceeded downstairs.

When they got to the town square, the other boarders were ready and waiting, and so was the bus. They loaded up once they were sure everyone was there, and soon, they were on their way. There was a lot of excited chatter on the bus, and people expressed their expectations of the town and shared memories of their last trip.

Nicole sat by the window seat, and with each discussion she listened in on, her excitement grew. She discovered that Leavenworth was in the mountains, and she was glad she'd packed for North Pole weather.

But when they arrived, she was in complete awe. The scene before her was mesmerizing. It was as if they'd walked into a snow globe. It was snowing lightly as if Mother Nature had just shaken the globe. The ground was covered in the fluffy white stuff, and the trees were dusted white with either all-white lights or green, orange, or purple— each one having a dominant color and lined the streets. The buildings were much of the same, with lights covering every space. One large tree stood in the center of town and was filled with green and red ornaments and twinkling lights. Even the fountain at the skating rink shot up white lights that crisscrossed each other in a glorious display.

"Oh...my...god!" Nicole gushed as she walked and soaked in the sights. "I've never seen anything like this."

"Incredible, isn't it?" Trisha asked.

"Who wants to go skating?" someone asked.

"Count me in," Nicole replied as a group of them walked over to get their rentals. Trisha decided she'd sit that one out. The booth was well-lit with yellow light and glowed red from the outside. Nothing was overlooked in that city of lights.

Nicole got her boots and slid around the ice stage with the other revelers, feeling very much like a kid again. When they stopped, Trisha pulled her over to where the life-sized characters were. "Let's get pictures with Frosty," she beamed. "And the nutcracker."

Nicole tagged along, and so did several others from town. There were elves and reindeer, several snowmen, Mrs. Claus, Santa Claus, and many more Christmas characters.

Carolers walked by them, circling the town and bringing even more Christmas cheer. The group stopped to get roasted chestnuts and hot cocoa before heading to the gazebo to listen to the choir as the carolers joined them in rounds of Christmas songs.

"They have a gingerbread competition like we do and a raffle for the town tree," Trisha told Nicole.

"This place feels like something out of a storybook. I'm glad I came."

"Me too," Trisha said as she took her hand and squeezed it. They remained with their hands locked for the rest of the performance before they retired for the night.

"I thought we were going shopping," a disappointed Nicole said to her mother when they entered their room.

It was also decorated with Christmas accessories—floor mats, garlands lining the room, red bows, stockings, and pine cones everywhere. There was even a Merry Christmas postcard on the entrance table.

"We can shop tomorrow before we go back home," Trisha told her. "Right now, I just want to get warm. I didn't realize how cold I was until I came in here." She rubbed her hands together before hugging herself. "I'm going to take a hot bath."

"I'm right behind you on that one," Nicole replied. "I wish there were two showers, and I didn't have to wait."

"I'll be quick," Trisha promised before she disappeared.

Nicole stood by the window, watching the fully lit town. It didn't seem as if there was any space that had been overlooked. And what was even better was that the lights never went out. She was well into the Christmas spirit once more.

As soon as her mother got out of the shower, Nicole took the opportunity to warm up with what felt like one of the best showers she'd ever gotten.

They were both wrapped in downy, soft robes, and they padded over to the sofa in front of the crackling fire. Trisha had just made more hot cocoa, which was just right. It was the perfect setting, with the soft light of the flames and the snow falling lightly outside the window.

"I'm glad we came," Nicole admitted as they cozied up by the fire. Things had been weird between her and her mom ever since she got back. She couldn't ignore the reason she'd left town, and it was out of guilt that she entertained her mother's every whim. But that night, she felt something more real— as if she was no longer pretending to smile.

"Me too," Trisha replied, then breathed in deeply right before she turned to Nicole. "It's really nice to have you back home. I've really missed you. And you just left, you know? Never looked back or hardly ever called. You were always too busy for a visit." Trisha sighed, then gently stroked Nicole's face.

Tears streamed down Nicole's face as she broke down

and collapsed onto her mother's shoulder. "I'm so sorry, Mom," she sobbed.

Nicole was tearing apart inside. She'd started to see things very differently since she returned home. All the memories, the people she'd met, the community she'd abandoned— they had all impacted her tremendously. It had been a lot to take in, and she wondered how her life would have been different, both for her and her daughter if she hadn't left Yuletide Creek.

"I didn't mean to just stay away," Nicole sniffled. "It's just that I've been so ashamed."

"What?" Trisha stopped her. "There is nothing to be ashamed of," Trisha wailed, looking incredulous. "What are you talking about?"

"It was all my fault," Nicole kept sobbing, and Trisha smoothed the side of her hair and held her closer. "And then I met Rudy, and you didn't want us to be together, and I hated that. So, when he and I got divorced, I knew you'd been right about him. And I didn't want to come back just to hear you say, *I told you so.*" She sighed. "And I knew you didn't really have to say it, but you'd be thinking it."

"Sweetheart, what do you mean by that? Do you really think that poorly of me? Why would I criticize you when my own marriage failed? You're my daughter."

"I know, but that's how I felt," Nicole replied softly.

Trisha started stroking her hair. "Honey, I could never judge you for a failed marriage. I didn't do so well in mine, just in case you didn't notice."

"I know, I know," Nicole said, then wiped her hand down her face. "I still feel partly responsible for that. Maybe I just gave him an excuse."

"What on earth are you going on about," Trisha asked, her brows knitted in confusion.

"Nothing." Nicole exhaled heavily, then lay in her mother's lap, staring at the fire as Trisha stroked her hair. She didn't want to go into the details. Maybe she should just let the past stay in the past. "Thanks, Mom," she sniffled, then wiped under her nose.

It had been a long time since she'd felt that close to her mother. They'd been separated for far too long, and she was glad she'd decided to return to Yuletide Creek.

"Speaking of which," Trisha said. "How's it going with Jake?"

Nicole blew out a breath. "I don't know. I thought it was going well, and then things got weird, so I don't know."

"Don't be too hard on him, sweetie," Trisha told her, still stroking her hair as she did. "He's been through a lot, and I suspect he's being cautious with you. Until he knows where your head is."

"Gee, Mom. I thought you'd be on my side," Nicole teased.

Trisha chuckled. "I am, which is why I want this to work. You deserve all the happiness in the world. Not to end up like me, and I think Jake...well, you know. You already like him."

"I know, he's a nice guy, but I just want to take it slow too. I'm not even sure why there's tension between us."

"Don't worry about it. Things will work out," Trisha replied. "In the meantime, what do you say we get some fresh cocoa and watch a couple of movies?"

Nicole sat up and stretched. "Why not? We have nothing better to do. And with everything going on all around us," she said, indicating the window, "it'd be an insult not to watch *Miracle on 34th Street*."

Trisha laughed. "Someone's really feeling the Christmas spirit."

"Yeah, guilty as charged. But how can I not?" Nicole asked while she spread her arms wide. "We're in Christmas town."

Trisha chuckled. "It's still my favorite time of year."

They refilled their hot cocoa, got some gingerbread cookies and holiday pudding, and snuggled up under the comfy throw as they prepared to watch the movie.

Chapter Fourteen

Nicole's eyes popped open as soon as the first streaks of light streamed in through the blinds.

Her heart started pounding as she leaped out of bed and threw her robe around her. The thick cotton swished around her calves as she scurried into the other room.

Stevie was already awake and sitting at the edge of the bed, one foot tucked under her and the other swinging as she stared at the screen on her phone. Her eyes rolled upward when she sensed her mother standing in the doorway.

"Mom, don't be creepy." She giggled.

Nicole laughed as she walked in. "I'm just so happy you're here now," she said, then joined her on the bed. She threw her arm around her shoulder, and Stevie put the phone down on the bed.

"Happy to see you, too, Mom, but we don't have to become Siamese twins while I'm here," she teased.

Stevie had arrived the day before, and Nicole had

experienced somewhat of an early Christmas when she had.

Nicole snickered, taking the hint. "Fine," she said, removing her arm. "But it's been just us for a while. Until you ditched me."

"Mom, I didn't ditch you. I went to college," she stated, rolling her eyes.

"Feels the same to me," Nicole moped.

"Well, in that case, I guess it runs in the family," she returned, then stuck out her tongue.

"Low blow," Nicole feigned disappointment. She still hadn't gotten over the fact that she's caused her parents' divorce and then had left town right after. It was a selfish move, but she wasn't thinking about that then.

Stevie laughed and grabbed her red hair at the top of her head, wrapping it into a messy bun. "Sorry, but you asked for it."

"Stevie? Nicole?" Trisha called from the hallway before she appeared.

"In here, Mom," Nicole replied.

Trisha was beaming when she walked into the room. "It's so good to see my two girls."

"Not you too, Grandma." Stevie smiled.

"Sue me," Trisha quipped. "I have breakfast downstairs, and then we have the tree to finish decorating."

"Oh, yes." Stevie grinned. "I forgot about that. Mom let's go," she exclaimed, jumping up. She was wearing pale green sweatpants, a matching shirt, and white cotton socks.

"Do I have to?" Nicole wailed. "I have to go to the shop, remember?"

"Jake will open up," Trisha told her as the three women walked out of Stevie's room.

"I still need to finish up what I was doing," Nicole told them as she made her way down the stairs.

"Stop the whining, honey, and let's just get it over with," Trisha scolded Nicole like a child.

Stevie giggled. "Yeah, Mom. It's just a tree. It doesn't bite."

"And we have to get this done soon too," Trisha told them, glancing back briefly as she walked. "The other carolers will be here in about two hours, so I don't have much time."

"Hey, maybe Mom can practice with you too," Stevie teased and covered her face as her mother shot her a dangerous look.

"If you keep this up, I'm going to have to return you to sender," Nicole said, pointing at Stevie.

"You two can bicker later." Trisha chuckled. "Stevie, can you make the popcorn?"

"Sure thing," Stevie said, then hurried off to the kitchen. "Oh, I smell blueberry pancakes," she shouted.

"Help yourself," Trisha called back and shuffled into the living room to sort out the rest of the Christmas decorations.

Nicole's face got sour right after she'd eaten her pancakes. She reluctantly started stringing popcorn as she watched Stevie and Trisha get tangled up in garland and tinsel.

"I can't believe this is how I'm spending my morning," Nicole grumbled to herself as she strung one popcorn kernel after another.

"Come on, Mom," Stevie argued as she threw a string of red tinsel at her. "Cheer up. How can you be so dull at a time like this?"

Trisha glanced over at her. "I thought visiting the Christmas town mellowed you a little."

"Maybe," Nicole sulked without looking at them. "I'm not all the way there yet," she told them, then got up. "And right now, it's past nine, and I should get to the shop."

Trisha waved her off. "Suit yourself. My grandbaby and I can handle this. By the time you get home, it should be done."

"And what's not done, you'll get to finish." Stevie grinned and wrapped gold tinsel around her neck. "Hey, maybe I can start this fashion trend."

Nicole rolled her eyes. "Glad to see you're both having fun. I'm about to have some of my own," she said sarcastically.

Stevie giggled. "See you later, Mom."

"Later, baby. Later Mom. Love you both," she told them and quickly made an exit.

She was warming up to Christmas again, but she wasn't fully reoriented just yet. She couldn't yet see herself skipping happily around a tree and going caroling. That part of her had died years ago.

But when she got to the shop, she wasn't sure if staying home and decorating the tree hadn't been the better option. Ever since her solo date night with Jake, things had been weird between them. Nicole still believed he'd overreacted, but she also remembered her mother asking her to take it easy on him. She didn't know exactly what hurt him outside of the small summary he'd given her, but she knew it was probably a whole lot more. So, she tried to ignore his sensitivity.

"Jake?" she called after she'd been there for almost

thirty minutes with nothing more than a chin-nod acknowledgment from him.

"Hmm?" he replied, slowly turning to her. "You need help with something?"

"Are we okay?" Nicole asked as she inched closer to him.

"What do you mean?" he asked, crossing his arms defensively across his chest.

"Like, things have been weird between us. Since that night when we went out, and I know you said..."

"Nicole," he interrupted, then leaned forward as he wore a crooked smile. "Don't sweat it. Nothing happened, and we're okay."

"Are you sure? Because you barely even talk to me anymore, and it's going to be very awkward if we have to work together all the time."

"I'm okay. You're okay. We're okay," Jake said nonchalantly. "Now, we still have stuff to do, so let's...let's just do that."

She wasn't sure she should believe him, that there was nothing wrong, but she sensed she wasn't going to get much out of him. She still wasn't sure what happened that night when he'd pretty much walked away, but he hadn't as much as complimented her ever since, much less ask her out on another date.

But she knew she just had to let it go, even though it bothered her that she didn't know what was wrong in the first place.

"All right," she said, then turned around in confusion. "So, I was wondering..."

"Here we go," Jake replied to her incomplete statement.

She laughed. "Whatever. Do you think the thieves found what they were looking for when they broke in?"

"I don't know," Jake said with an exasperated sigh.

"I don't think they did," Nicole stated excitedly, then turned to the large bookcase in the corner.

"Please don't tell me you still want to get into the root cellar," Jake said wearily. "We can't even get it open."

"Because we never really tried," Nicole told him and walked quickly to the back of the room. "Can you please move this?"

"You're relentless, you know that?" He smirked as he inched closer.

She turned to look at all six feet of him, dressed in a black cotton T-shirt with gray thermal covering the rest of his arm and black jeans. She wasn't sure how he did it, but he could make burlap look good.

"Curiosity is killing me," she admitted and stood aside for him to move the furniture off the latch on the floor.

"Have at it," he told her.

"You really want me to try opening it alone?" she asked him incredulously.

He crossed his arms. "Well, we tried last time, and it didn't work, so I'm not sure what you want me to do this time."

She shook her head and walked back to the office in search of any tool she could find that could help her. She found a wrench and a pair of scissors.

Jake laughed when he saw her returning with them. "Yeah, those will help," he mocked.

Nicole ignored him and went to work, but it didn't matter what she did; the latch wouldn't budge.

Jake got tired of watching her. "Fine!" he shot out,

then got down on the floor next to her. "Here, let me try again," he said, grabbing for the wrench.

"It's okay," Nicole said stubbornly. "I can do it."

"Just give me the thing," Jake insisted, gripping it. "You can't...even...open...it," he struggled to say as he practically forced the wrench from Nicole's hand.

"No," she replied, trying to force the wrench down on the latch. She knew she could do it, and she didn't want him getting the credit for what she found.

"This is insane," Jake said. "Clearly, you can't open it."

"I can," she returned obstinately and pulled on the wrench so hard it caused Jake to lose his balance, falling onto his wrist.

She realized what she'd done as soon as she'd done it. She gasped as the wrench clattered to the ground, and Jake tipped over onto his bum, holding his wrist and clenching his jaw.

"Jake, I'm so sorry," she apologized, then clambered over to him. "Let me see."

She wouldn't stop until she had her way, so he reluctantly held his hand out to her. "Happy?"

"No." She sighed. "Looks like it might be fractured. Come on, let's get you to the clinic."

"I'll be fine," Jake told her, then shook her off as he tried to stand. The pain was obviously greater than he realized, and his hand hung limp like a ragdoll.

"Yeah," she said, rolling her eyes. "I can see that. Just come on."

Jake ground his teeth together. "Okay, okay," he relented.

Nicole felt awful about the fact that she'd hurt him,

and she still hadn't gotten the latch free. She locked up the shop and hurriedly drove him to the clinic.

The clinic resembled every other house and shop in Yuletide Creek. There was a red and green wreath on the main door with pine cones and ribbons attached to it, strings of light running around the frame of the building, two large candy canes on either side of the door, and snowflakes on the windows. She couldn't escape Christmas in Yuletide Creek.

A large Christmas tree awaited them in the lobby, filled with shiny red, green, and blue ornaments, bells, and ribbons, and the reception desk was laid with garlands and red and white stockings.

"Good morning," the receptionist wearing a Santa hat beamed and greeted them as they entered.

"Hey," Nicole replied. "He needs to get his wrist checked. He might've sprained it."

"You mean you might've sprained it," Jake countered softly so only she could hear, and she blushed.

"Right away," the receptionist said. "Just register on the machine over there, and someone will see you as soon as possible."

"Thanks," Jake mumbled, then walked off.

One look around the waiting room told Nicole they might be there for a while. "Seems they're a bit short-staffed," she muttered.

"That's right," a woman to her right said. "I've been waiting here for thirty minutes now." She fixed her shawl around her shoulders. Her graying hair peeked from under the scarf she wore, and her eyes revealed laugh lines that forced a smile onto Nicole's face too.

"Wow," Nicole replied as a woman and child walked in. "Looks like it might be a long day."

"You can say that again," the woman said. "You might as well get comfortable," she told her and nodded at the stack of magazines on the glass-top coffee table.

A thought came to her, and she got up and walked over to the receptionist. "Say, how long will the wait be?"

"Uh, maybe an hour?" she asked and cocked her head to the side. "I'm really sorry, but we're short of qualified staff at this clinic, and lord knows we've tried."

"I see," Nicole told her as her heart began to pound heavily. She could easily lend her expertise to the clinic. She'd do a lot of good, and she'd have much more pleasant people to work with.

"If you know anyone, point them in our direction," she told Nicole.

"Will do," Nicole responded, then walked back to her seat.

"What was that about?" Jake asked when she returned.

"I was just checking how long we'd wait," she told him, leaving out the part about her possible new career path.

But the woman hadn't been wrong— they waited for fifty minutes before Jake was finally seen. It was only a mild sprain, so they wrapped his wrist, and was told to take it easy for a while.

"I have an idea," Jake said when they stepped outdoors again.

"What?" she asked.

"With all this Christmas cheer around me, let's go caroling," he suggested.

And Nicole's jaw dropped.

Chapter Fifteen

"**Y**ou must be joking," she told him.

"I'm not." Jake laughed.

"I thought you wouldn't want anything to do with me after causing you an injury. I wasn't expecting to be invited caroling."

Jake chuckled. "I know you didn't mean to," he told her with a sympathetic look. "But you still owe me."

"Not that much," Nicole protested as they got to her car. "I mean, come on. Caroling? I can't even sing even if I was into this whole Christmas thing."

"Doesn't matter," Jake countered. "You can stand in the back. Lip sync." He grinned.

"Nope," she moaned, then shook her head vehemently. "I'd never live that down with Stevie either."

Jake snickered. "You're going to miss out on a whole lot of Christmas cheer," Jake told her. "Plus," he said, holding up his injured hand, "you owe me."

Nicole groaned. Christmas caroling was the last thing on the list of things to do at Christmas that she saw herself doing. In fact, she wasn't sure how her mother even got into caroling— she was just as tone-deaf as Nicole. She would feel like so much of a hypocrite, hating Christmas so much while knocking on doors, spreading "cheer." She couldn't do it.

"Look, I'll drop you off somewhere, and you can go caroling," she told Jake as she drove back to the shop. "You can ask me to do anything else. Lick the floors of the shop even. But no caroling."

Jake's voice boomed as he chortled heartily. "You'd rather lick the shop floor clean than sing? That's easier?"

"Yes!" she said resolutely.

"Okay, how about you don't do it for me and do it for your mother instead?" he asked.

She turned briefly to look at him. "My mother?"

"Yeah," he said and threw his hands up. "I mean, she has looked forward to you coming for a long time. All she talked about was you, and I know how much Christmas means to her. Just imagine how she'd feel if you showed up. If even to just support her."

She squinted her eyes at him. "That's cheating."

He chuckled. "What is?"

"You're using my mother to strong-arm me into the worst extracurricular activity ever," she fumed.

He laughed and wagged his brows at her. "Did it work?"

She grunted at him and didn't respond. How could she say no? She owed her mother to not ruin Christmas for her. She promised herself she'd try her best, and it'd only be two more weeks, more or less. She could hold out a little longer.

"Yes!" she hissed. "But this isn't pay for your wrist. For this, you owe me big time!"

Jake snickered. "All right then. You'll love it."

"And you claimed you were indifferent to Christmas. What a load of bull, and I fell for it," she complained to herself, much to Jake's amusement. "I'm glad you think this is funny."

He was still laughing. "Turn left up here," he said, indicating Madison Avenue. "They might be up here or will be passing soon."

Nicole didn't respond. She was just dreading the door-to-door visitation. She grew even more anxious when she saw Jake was right. "I guess you know their route."

"Yep," he told her and pulled the car over. "Come on. Let's catch up."

Nicole felt even worse when she saw Stevie was there with her mother. "Oh, god, shoot me now," she muttered to Jake.

"What?" he asked with a laugh.

"My daughter is going to have a field day with this," Nicole told him as her face grew bright red.

"Mom?" Stevie asked when she spotted Nicole. "What are you doing here?"

"Don't!" Nicole told her before she started giggling.

"What did I tell you? You owe me ten dollars!" Stevie teased, holding her hand out. "Pay up."

Nicole cringed and reached into her purse for the ten dollars. "Here!" she said grudgingly, then pointed at Jake with a menacing look before she walked off.

"Thanks," she heard Stevie whisper to Jake, and Nicole smiled a little.

"You're welcome, but it was really hard," Jake whispered back.

Nicole stopped and turned. "I don't think either of you know how whispering works."

They both laughed before Stevie skipped up to her and looped her hand through hers. "It's fun, Mom. You'll get the hang of it."

"I doubt it," Nicole replied.

But she soon ate her words. The first door they stopped at on Madison, they sang "Silver Bells" and then "Joyful, Joyful, We Adore Thee." Nicole wasn't familiar with the second, but she found herself humming along to the other songs that she knew.

Stevie looked over at her and grinned when she caught her humming to "O Come All Ye Faithful" and "Away in a Manger."

"Stop looking at me like I'm an alien," she warned her.

Trisha laughed. "Not so bad, is it?"

"I'm not talking to any of you," Nicole told them, even though she had to admit she was enjoying herself. If even a little bit. The smiles that spread on the faces of the people who greeted them at the door and the little girl in the wheelchair whose eyes became glossy because she couldn't go out like the other children— it was enough to tear up even the hardest heart.

"How many houses are we going to visit?" Nicole asked after what felt like their hundredth stop.

"We just have one more street," Trisha replied, "and then we stop for hot cocoa and gingerbread cookies."

"Goody," Nicole said, widening her eyes in mock satisfaction.

"Mom, behave." Stevie giggled.

Jake threw his arm around her. "Come on. I saw you getting into it. Don't pretend you don't like it."

She wanted to tell him that the best part of the day

thus far was then— when he had his arm around her shoulder, and she felt as if she was his girl.

Then he brought his lips to her ear. "I knew there was a little bit of Christmas spirit in there."

She blushed and held her head down, all too conscious about the way his arm rested so comfortably against her. But then the mood was quickly shot down when she looked up and saw her mother grinning at her like a Cheshire cat.

She cleared her throat and reached over to Stevie. "I didn't take you for a caroler."

She shrugged just as Jake's hand slipped from Nicole's shoulder. "I wasn't, but hey, when in Rome, right?"

"I guess so," Nicole agreed reluctantly.

Jake didn't leave her side for a minute for the rest of the walk, and she was so conscious about it that she was mindful of every step she took and everything she said. She was nervous yet excited, and she wondered if he'd finally come around again.

On more than one occasion, she felt his hand brushing against hers, and she wanted desperately for him to take her hand. She wanted him to lead and not to be the one who was too forward.

When they stopped for hot cocoa at one of the carolers' homes, Trisha and Stevie went inside as Nicole and Jake remained outdoors.

"It's not such a bad day," Nicole commented as she looked around. "Not too cold."

"Yeah, today was awesome," Jake replied. "Minus my almost broken hand."

Nicole laughed. "You're not going to let go of that, are you?"

"Nope." He grinned, and his dark brown eyes sparkled at her. "I figure you should spend a lot more time trying to make it up to me."

"Is that so?" she asked as her heart started to race again.

"It is so." He smiled as he brushed her hair behind her ear.

Nicole saw her mother coming from inside the house, and immediately she felt the urge to step away from Jake. He noticed it, too, and gazed at her.

"You do know your mom is rooting for us, right?" he asked.

"I know," she told her. "Let's get some cocoa."

"All right," he said, holding out his hand so she could go first.

She could feel his gaze on her the entire time they walked to get their cups. They started walking and talking, and Nicole wasn't sure when they separated from everyone else and were alone on the back porch. The other carolers had either left or were inside the house.

Jake leaned against the beam at the top of the back steps with his cup still in hand as he stared at her.

"What?" she asked when she caught him.

"I'm really glad you came after all," he told her. "I know you're not into all of this Christmas stuff, but I know it meant a lot to your mom."

"Only my mom?" she asked and stepped closer to him.

He smiled. "And to Stevie," he teased.

She laughed as she stood in front of him. "Yeah, I know."

He took a deep breath and looked past her. "I don't have the best memories of Christmas either, but this town," he said, then sucked in a deep breath, "there's something magical about being here. It's like no problem is too great that Yuletide Creek can't fix."

"I know what you mean," Nicole agreed. "I came here with a lot of baggage. Planned to just pass through quickly— help Mom with the shop and be gone in a week. But the longer I'm here, it's like..."

"The less you want to leave," he finished for her. "I know. I've got the bug too."

"What's the cure for that?" she asked him.

"Stay," he told her as he reached out to take her hand. "Whatever you need, you can find it here."

She bit her lower lip and stared deeply into his eyes before she threw her head back and closed her eyes. "I can't believe this. I didn't come here for all of this."

"Me neither. But it found us," he told her.

She opened her eyes, and they caught the sprig of mistletoe that was attached to the garland between the beams. "Oh, look. A mistletoe."

The words were barely out of her mouth when Jake leaned forward, touched her waist lightly, and gently pressed his lips to hers.

Nicole's eyes popped. She wasn't expecting that, but as his lips slid against hers, she slowly gave in to him and looped her hand around his neck.

It was as if she'd been waiting for that moment for a long time, but now that it was there, she began to have doubts and reservations.

His kiss was sweet, but the effects of it were nothing that Nicole could have anticipated.

Chapter Sixteen

"This is so stupid!" she chided herself as she stared at her reflection in the mirror the following morning. "It was just one kiss."

But the one kiss had her head in circles. She didn't know what to make of it. She wasn't sure if she was ready for a full-blown relationship. In fact, she wasn't even sure Jake was ready for that either. She didn't want to read too much into the kiss, but it was impossible to think it was just a casual encounter, either.

"I'm so screwed," she told herself before she splashed water onto her face. She wasn't sure how she was going to face Jake. What if he wanted something she couldn't give? She wasn't even sure she wanted to stay in town.

She eventually left the bathroom, going as slowly as she could, and got dressed in a pair of leggings and an oversized sweater. A pair of black thigh-high boots and a scarf completed her look, but she felt as if she was all dressed up with nowhere to go.

"What's the matter, dear?" her mother asked her when she noticed her hesitancy.

"Nothing," Nicole blurted out, which didn't help her case.

"You sure seem agitated. Anything I can help with?"

Nicole stared at her blankly for a couple of minutes. "No. Of course not. You and Stevie have plans for today, right?"

"Yes. We're going to check out some of the displays in Brunswick."

"Good for you. I hope you have fun," Nicole told her, then picked up her laptop. "See you later."

Her mother was still looking at her in a weird way as she left the house. She couldn't blame her. She sat in the car for a couple of minutes before she drove off, but she didn't head for the store. She wasn't ready to face Jake yet. She figured she could hole up in the library and do some research on some of the items in the store. Some of them were more valuable than she realized and would need proper insurance.

She had a legitimate reason for not going into the store, and just so he would worry, she sent Jake a very generic text that she'd be doing some research on a few items and hoped he wouldn't show up at the library to check up on her. There was no way she could hide all the confusion in her heart. Not from him— she sensed he was very intuitive.

She got to the library, carrying a cup of coffee with her, and found a cozy little section in the back where she was least likely to be disturbed. She set the computer down and pulled up the list of items she needed clarity on.

She was barely on the second item, poring over notes on the internet and trying to pull up an image that resembled it when she saw a dark shadow come over her screen.

She sputtered her coffee when she saw that it was Alan. She scrunched up her face and spread her arms. "What now?"

He pulled up a chair, once again, inviting himself to her table. "I come in peace."

"When have you ever?" she asked. "Look, I'm really busy right now. I don't have the time for any of your nonsense."

"What nonsense?" he asked as he sat back in the chair. "Nicole, I'm only interested in one thing."

"I bet you are," she replied suggestively.

He knitted his brows. "I beg your pardon? What does that mean?"

"It means I know it was you," she accused, pointing the end of her pen at him.

"It was me with what?" he asked, appearing genuinely ignorant.

"The store," she blurted out, then lowered her voice when she remembered where she was. "What, because Mom wouldn't sell, so you decided you'd trash the place instead?"

"What on earth?" he asked. "I'm afraid I don't know what you're talking about."

"Your little innocent game doesn't work with me. Am I supposed to believe that you weren't the one who tore through the shop looking for God knows what? Breaking the shop glass in the process and costing my mother unnecessary money?"

He sighed. "I'm sure the shop was insured, so the insurance would pay for that," he said before he realized how guilty he sounded. "I didn't mean it like that. I'm just saying it didn't really cost her any money, but I'm wounded that you thought I had anything to do with that."

"Wounded?" she scoffed. "Like I care."

"Look, I just came over here to ask if you'd thought about taking me up on my offer to sell the place."

"I already told you flat out, no. Now, after what you did..." she said, shaking her head, "there's no way in hell we would ever sell to you."

"Look, why would I want to trash a place I want to buy?" He leaned forward, trying to make sense, his perfect white teeth glistening. He was dressed in a navy suit with a sky-blue shirt and no tie. It must have been a dress-down day at work.

"I don't know how scumbags think. Maybe you wanted to convince my mother that the place wasn't worth the foundation it sat on. Maybe she'd throw in the towel and fold." Nicole leaned forward as well so she was within inches of Alan's smug face. "It's not happening. The place isn't for sale, so you can just crawl back into that hole you were hiding in before you came to Yuletide."

"Isn't that why you're here, though? To convince her it isn't worth the trouble?"

Nicole pulled back, shocked at his words. "You seem to know an awful lot about me and my mother for someone who just came to town."

"Whatever," Alan replied, then sat back so hard the chair scraped under his weight. Then he abruptly stood again. "And you know what's funny?"

She sat back, too, and crossed her arms over her chest. "No, but I'm sure you're gonna tell me."

"The danger is right under your nose, and you don't even know it," he scoffed, and she wrinkled her brows. "If you need to worry about someone, how about looking a little closer to home."

"What on earth are you talking about?" Nicole asked.

"If anyone wants you to sell out of fear, it's Jake!"

"Jake?" Nicole asked, scrunching her face in confusion. "Are you crazy? Jake loves that store as much as we do. If not more."

"I bet he does," Alan shot. "He's a snake."

Nicole gawked, and then a laugh ripped from her so loudly it caught the attention of the passing librarian. "Sorry," she apologized. "Do you even hear yourself? Do you want me to believe that Jake is trying to undermine my mother? Jake?"

It sounded even more insane the more she thought about it. All she could see was Jake's sweet face— a picture of decency and kindness. He'd have to be the greatest con in history to have fooled her into thinking he was someone she could fall for. Had fallen for, and the blush rose to her cheeks before she had a chance to disguise it.

"Aw, you're sweet on him, aren't you?" Alan teased.

"Look, when Jake found out you were sniffing around and asking to sell, he was livid."

"Of course he was," Alan snarled. "He was worried that I'd be cutting him out of the commission."

"What commission? Jake isn't a salesman," Nicole protested, even as she fought to believe that Jake was innocent.

Alan sniffled and wiped his hand under his nose. "Okay, I know you won't believe me without some proof, so," he told her as he took out his phone. "Here. Have a look at this."

"I don't want to see some made-up story of the lies

you've been spinning," Nicole said, rejecting his suggestion.

"You want to know or not?" Alan persisted.

Curiosity got the better of Nicole, and she took the phone from Alan. "I don't know what you expect me to see here," she said, tapping the screen. She saw a row of email messages between Jake and Alan. Alan was pitching his idea of the sale of the store, and Jake told him to leave it up to him— he'd handle it and not let the old lady or her daughter know about it. Alan told him that if he could make it happen, he would keep it between them, but Jake said the only way he would is if he could get forty percent of the commission.

"I don't believe it," Nicole replied, shaking her head, then she pushed the phone back to him. "This doesn't sound like Jake."

"Hey," Alan said, then took his phone back. "You wanted proof, so I gave you proof. It's up to you if you want to believe it or not. But think about this— why do you think he acted out when he heard from you that I was trying to buy?"

"He was just as disgusted as the rest of us," Nicole countered, continuing to defend Jake even though the doubt was slowly working its way into her consciousness.

"That's what he wants you to believe. Jake doesn't care about that shop. He barely makes any money working there. As soon as I approached him, he was on board with it."

"That doesn't make any sense," Nicole argued, fighting the suspicions. "Why would you even go to him?"

"Because of this," he said, pointing between them. "Look at the reception I got from you. I figured it would be better to approach the man."

"Still, I don't see Jake selling us out just for a few bucks," Nicole told him.

"Try a couple hundred thousand." Alan grinned. "Think he would do it for that?"

"Impossible," she hissed as if she'd been stung. Instantly her mind started replaying all the conversations she'd had with Jake. Maybe he wasn't trying hard enough to get into the root cellar because he had other plans for what was down there. Maybe he had been playing her all along, and he was just biding his time. But how would selling the shop guarantee he'd get anything that might be in the root cellar? He knew a lot more about the business and the shop than she did, and he'd gained her mother's trust completely.

Nothing made sense to her, but she wasn't about to let Alan believe that he'd spooked her. *Who knew?* Maybe he was the one who was trying to manipulate her, and she hated the fact that she couldn't tell one from the other.

But she smiled and looked over at Alan even though secretly she was devastated by what he'd shared with her. She'd seen the proof in the emails. There was no way Jake could deny it. But she didn't have to give Alan the satisfaction that he'd won.

"I think that's enough for today," she told him. "We're still not selling. Jake can't sell or get commission without us, so you best be on your way now," she advised, then shooed him.

Alan shook his head, clearly frustrated. "Don't say I didn't warn you," he blurted out as he slipped his phone into his pocket and walked off.

Nicole took a deep breath, trying to calm her rapid beating heart. Her eyes burned with tears that threatened to fall as waves of betrayal washed over her. She couldn't understand why Jake would betray her mother like that. A moment later, she wiped her hand down her face.

She'd lost all focus, so she closed the computer screen. She wasn't going to the shop anymore. She couldn't face Jake for more than one reason, and she couldn't go home either. She wasn't sure how much of what she'd found out she should tell her mother or if she should tell her anything at all.

It would eat her alive to know about Jake's betrayal. But even Nicole knew she couldn't take the word of a conman on blind faith. Even though she'd seen the proof, she still harbored a little faith that Jake was a victim, but the more the messages played over in her mind, the more jaded she became.

Jake had played her. Royally! And almost won.

Chapter Seventeen

There wasn't much Nicole could do for the rest of the day.

She managed to scramble through a couple of research articles, and she found two images to support one item, but for the most part, her day was wasted. She left the library at three and drove home.

She was hoping that her mom and Stevie wouldn't have returned yet, and her heart galloped when she saw her suburban in the driveway.

She sighed and pulled up beside it, grabbing her files and laptop as she exited her car. Nicole smelled something delicious as she stepped inside the back door, and Trisha's head peeped out from the kitchen.

"Hey, what are you doing here so early?" Trisha asked with curious eyes.

"I was doing some research, but I got tired, so I figured I'd finish here. What are you cooking?" she asked as she tried to change the subject.

Trisha's brows dipped. "You're sure it's just that?"

"Yep," Nicole replied, then hurried off. She didn't

want to be under her mother's scrutinizing glare.

She remained upstairs and hoped that her mother wouldn't bother her or demand questions. She didn't, and she realized afterward that she hadn't heard Stevie either — maybe she'd found some friends and was out. It was just as well with Nicole— she didn't want to lie to either of them. Or both.

But when her stomach started growling, she knew it was time for her to come out of hibernation. She treaded cautiously down the steps, peering around her for signs of her mother. Both she and Stevie had done a great job with the decorations— the tree in the living room was all blue, white, and silver. The garland that was weaved through the banister boasted twinkling white lights and red poinsettia leaves wrapped around them. There were candy canes and stockings hanging from doorknobs and the fireplace, and lights ran around the living room and along the passage to the kitchen.

"Nicole? Is that you?" Trisha called from the living room.

Nicole sighed. She wasn't moving as stealthily as she thought. "Yes, Mom?" she asked.

"I thought you were sleeping. That's why I didn't come up there. Come in here a second," she said.

Nicole's shoulders sagged as she walked to the living room. "What is it?" she asked as she stopped just short of the room and poked her head around the corner.

Trisha grinned and held up a knitted red-and-green sweater with a large Christmas hat in the middle. "What do you think?" Trisha asked as she held it up.

"Uh, that's not mine, is it?"

Trisha laughed. "No, this one is mine. *This* is yours," she informed, holding up another sweater that was pretty much the same but was striped green and red with a smiling Santa Claus on the front.

"No, thank you," Nicole replied, shaking her head.

"Come on," Trisha goaded as she stood up. "I'm sure it's the right size," she said as she came up to Nicole and measured it against the front of her chest. "See?"

"Mom, I wouldn't be caught dead in that," Nicole told her.

"But that's the whole point. We could win. It's an ugly sweater party the Millers are having."

"Well, that's bound to win a prize, but not on me," Nicole told her as she walked off again toward the kitchen.

"Come on, don't be such a spoiled sport," Trisha lamented as she scurried after Nicole. "It's not going to kill you."

Nicole sighed. "Mom, I just don't want to go, okay?" She sighed again. "What's for dinner?"

Trisha's brows dipped as she surveyed her daughter. "Something's wrong. What's going on?"

"Nothing," Nicole lied as she tried to avoid her eyes. She knew what Alan told her was a lie, but until she either confronted Jake about it or found some more fool-proof evidence, she wasn't willing to share the information just yet. For all she knew, it could still be a misunderstanding, and she didn't want to break the relationship between her mother and Jake if it wasn't necessary.

Trisha exhaled. "Is this about Jake?" she asked pointedly.

Nicole sputtered on the water she'd just started drinking. *Is it that obvious?* "What?" she asked, wiping her backhand over her mouth.

"I see how you two have been carrying on and that he's getting smitten with you. But don't you play with that man, honey," she warned. "If you don't want anything serious with him, don't string him along. His heart's too big to be someone's plaything."

"Mom, I'm not doing that," Nicole told her. "And by the way, I can get hurt, too, you know," she reminded her. In fact, for all she knew, she was the one being played. If Jake was who Alan said he was, then it wasn't his heart her mother needed to be worrying about.

"I know that, honey, but I also know you're tougher than he is." She smiled as she pinched Nicole's cheek. "He's a darling, that's what he is."

She was so tempted at that moment to tell her mother that Jake may not be who she thought he was, but she held her tongue.

"It has nothing to do with Jake, okay?" she lied, then turned away, so her mother wouldn't see the truth in her eyes.

"Oh?" Trisha asked, following her. "What is it then?"

"Mom," she returned, raising her voice but then sighed. "It's just that this time of year affects me in ways no other time does, so I'm just wrestling with memories and trying not to think about certain things."

"Aw, honey," Trisha said as her face dropped, and so did her hands. "I'm so sorry." She sighed.

"It's okay, Mom," she replied. She had chosen the worst possible topic to get out of telling her mother about Jake. Once she'd mentioned her Christmas ghosts, they came knocking, and soon, she started to feel the effects of it too.

It didn't matter how many garlands she hung or how many carols or gingerbread cookies she helped to bake.

None of that did anything to assuage the guilt she still felt over the fact that her parents got divorced because of her.

"I know it's hard when you have to separate because of a divorce, but when it happens during the holidays, it's especially hard. And I should know."

Nicole's eyes watered, and she looked away instantly as she choked back the tears. "Mom, I'm so sorry," she sobbed.

"Nicole? What on earth?" Trisha asked in surprise, walking around to her front. "What are you sorry for? What happened?"

"You could have been happy still and not have spent so many years alone if it weren't for me," Nicole said, looking up at the ceiling in a vain attempt to keep her tears at bay.

"What do you mean if it weren't for you?" Trisha asked, gripping her forearms. "Talk to me, child!" she said sternly as if Nicole was ten again.

Nicole could see the panic in her eyes, but her heart was aching from the pain that she'd carried for years.

"What are you sorry for? Is it the shop? Did something happen?"

"No, Mom. I'm sorry for causing you and Dad divorcing," she murmured softly.

"You're what?" Trisha asked in disbelief.

"I know I was the one who caused it, okay?" Nicole blurted out.

"Oh, honey. My sweet, sweet girl," Trisha consoled as she tried to reason with her daughter. "How could you think that you caused your father and I to get a divorce?"

"Because I was the one who took the car out for a joyride and totaled it, even though dad told me not to. I heard all the arguments, how dad kept telling you that

144

you coddled me too much, and how you told him that he was the one who taught me to drive in the first place." She sighed, then wiped her hand down her face.

The look on her mother's face was one of dismay. It clearly showed on her mother's face that she hadn't known that Nicole knew about the fighting or had thought she'd been the catalyst for their divorce. But it had been too much for her to bear over the years.

"You guys fought about everything after that," Nicole sniffled, no longer hungry for the dinner she'd come downstairs for. "From what to eat to who would take me to school or what would happen once I left school. Everything. And I never heard it that much until I wrecked the car."

"Honey," Trisha murmured, then took her hand. "Come here." She led her back to the living room. "You and I have never had this talk before, but it's high time." She sighed. "You did not cause the divorce. That was a long time coming."

Nicole's brows furrowed. "What do you mean? You guys had a strong marriage before that night."

"That's what you think," Trisha told her. "I don't know where your dad and I went wrong, but we went wrong a long time ago. There were many nights we didn't even sleep in the same bed. We always put on a show, so to speak, for you. We did right by you— kept you in the dark. It's also why we never had any more children— we didn't want to bring any more children into that marriage. Somehow, we knew it would be over soon."

"But, Mom," Nicole tried as memories flashed before her eyes. "All the birthday parties? Family trips? Those were just fake?"

Trisha sucked in a lungful of air. "Not fake, sweetie.

It's not like we never had any real memories or any good times. There were moments when we thought we would make it, but more times than not, we knew that was just wishful thinking. So, that night when you had the accident, it was probably the straw that broke the camel's back," she explained, reaching out to stroke her daughter's cheek.

Nicole closed her eyes and leaned into her mother's open palm, holding it to her face as tears cascaded down her cheeks. "I thought that I..."

"Is that why you left? Why you never came back to visit?" Trisha asked her, her eyebrows cocked.

Nicole shook her head yes. "I couldn't bear to look at you while knowing what I'd done."

Trisha's eyes grew glossy as she reached in and hugged her daughter. "Oh, my dear child," she sobbed. "What did we do?"

"I don't know," Nicole cried into her mother's shoulder.

"All this time, you stayed away because you felt guilty?" Trisha pulled back and asked. "And I didn't even know. It was all a lie, baby," she said as she wiped Nicole's tears away. "You could never bring me that much pain. You, my child, were the only joy I ever had. You truly have to believe that, Nicole. You are my everything."

Nicole fell against her chest as Trisha smoothed her hair. "I'm sorry, Mom. I should have said something sooner. I should have come to you."

"It's okay, honey. Better late than never," Trisha told her. "And to think of how many Christmases you lost because of that. How many we lost. Well, no more. Now we know the truth, so we can do something about it this time."

"Yes. No more lost time between us," Nicole said as she wiped her tear-stained face that looked a lot like her mother's.

"What'd I miss?" Stevie asked as she walked into the room.

"Nothing," they both replied at the same time, then burst into laughter.

"Are you two okay?" Stevie asked, raising her brow.

"Never better," Trisha replied as she pinched Nicole's cheek. "Now, what do you say we have a Christmas none of us will ever forget?"

"I'm already having that," Nicole told her, smiling. "And you're not getting me in that ugly sweater."

Trisha laughed. "Darn it! I thought for sure that would work."

"Maybe Stevie wouldn't mind wearing it." Nicole snickered, then thumbed at the sweater her grandmother held up.

"Uh, I'm not *that* into Christmas," she returned, then backed away. "Count me out."

"I can't believe I'm related to either of you." Trisha sulked. "Fine. I'll go by myself."

"Fine by me." Nicole grinned as she watched her mother stomp upstairs, trying hard to guilt her into going with her.

She literally felt the weight lifting from her shoulders. For so long, she'd carried pain that wasn't real. If she'd only said it to her mother years ago, they'd have saved themselves so much.

But that only solved one problem. She still had Jake to worry about, and something told her that resolution would be a messy one.

Chapter Eighteen

Trisha tried to get Nicole to go to the party with her and Stevie, but she was firm in her refusal. Trisha had finally guilt-tripped Stevie so much that she'd finally relented.

"Okay, your loss," Trisha told her as they both walked through the door, looking as if Christmas had thrown up on them.

"I'm sure it is," Nicole replied, plopping down onto the sofa.

Now that she and her mother had resolved the age-old nothing that had kept them apart, she was lighter than she'd been in years. She sat on the sofa with her laptop next to her. And the remote.

Maybe she could have a quiet evening, watch a movie with a glass of wine and settle into her own skin again. But as soon as she turned on the TV, she knew she'd made a mistake. It was all Santa and jolliness, so much so that she wanted to puke.

It didn't help that she had a red-and-green throw draped across her legs, the Christmas lights were flickering in the background, and the house smelled like cinnamon and pine. She might have resolved things with her mother, but she still wasn't all the way in with Christmas just yet.

"Okay, that's it," she said to know one, then tossed the throw behind her as she got up. If she heard Rudolph's name one more time, she was going to go postal.

She checked the time and saw that it was a quarter to nine. She didn't want to stay inside the house anymore, and she didn't want to participate in any jingle-bell activities. Her best bet was to go to the shop and finish what she'd started. There was still so much to do. Hopefully, she would get more done while she was in the shop while she wasn't surrounded by all the chaos— maybe it would inspire her.

The shop wasn't looking like the inside of a pinata anymore, which made her feel as if her time in Yuletide Creek wasn't altogether wasted.

Nicole was glad when she pulled up to the shop and saw the closed sign on the door. She sighed with relief— she wouldn't have to face Jake yet.

She got out and slipped her files under her arm, and gripped her laptop. She opened the door and sucked in a deep breath as she walked inside. She walked to the little office and set her laptop down, plopping down in the seat behind it.

It was then she noticed how the office was not as neat and orderly as she would have wanted it to be. She set about to clean it. She sorted the files in and on the single cabinet in the corner. Then, she emptied out the drawers, placing the stationeries in one and notepads and Post-its in another.

Nicole could tell she was probably procrastinating, but the store wasn't acting as an inspiration at all.

She fell back into her seat when she couldn't find anything else to fix. She picked up her phone and called Stevie.

"Bored much?" Stevie asked.

"You can say that again," Nicole replied, toying with the pen in her hand as she swiveled the chair.

"Where are you? You can still come by. You don't have to be wearing an ugly sweater or anything."

Nicole exhaled, then fell back into the chair. "No, I'm good. I'm at the shop, trying to see if I can get anything done, but it's not working."

"Yeah, because that's all you do, even your body is protesting," Stevie told her.

Nicole chuckled. "Maybe, but I still need to get this shop worthy of anyone's attention. Enjoy the party. I just wanted to check in on you."

"Okay," Stevie replied and hung up, leaving Nicole with nothing but her thoughts again.

Nicole twirled some more in the seat before she flew up and walked into the shop. She didn't want to turn the lights on and spook people in town who might think someone was breaking in again. Or maybe just her with a flashlight would have the same effect.

She decided she'd go with the lights. Her eyes caught the cash register, and she wondered if Jake had cleaned it out. She wandered over to it and realized he hadn't emptied it out. She shook her head and started to do that. When she was done, she found some other menial tasks to do. Everything but what she'd planned to do when she got there.

"This is insane," Nicole said to herself when she

made it back to the office. She hadn't cataloged one item, and it wasn't that it was hard— she just wasn't in the mood for it.

She groaned and covered her face with her palm. She started opening drawers again, and her eyes caught the old jewelry box inside it.

"Oh, I almost forgot about you," she said to the box, then picked it up. She turned it over in her hands, checking out the strange markings on it. "I bet you were a thing of beauty when you were first made."

She turned it over as she tried to figure out who might have made it. If she could find a newer one, she wouldn't have to keep that old one. She couldn't find anything. Whatever distinguishing mark there was from the maker had aged out. She started to get excited that it could be a one-of-a-kind item, but with nothing to tell her anything about it, how could she even prove that?

An internet search for another couple of minutes didn't help either. There was no jewelry box like it on the internet. She even took pictures of it, but nothing turned up.

"You're quite the mystery, aren't you?" she asked it. But with nothing to go on, she set it down on the desk, knowing she'd come back to it later.

It was sort of bent out of shape, but the way the markings were so intricately designed, from what she could make out, she knew that a lot of love and attention had been given to it. It didn't belong with the rest of the junk that she was going to throw out.

Which gave her another idea— the latch.

She grabbed her screwdriver and marched into the store. She was able to pull away the furniture from over the latch, and she stooped to survey it more. Maybe she'd been trying the wrong way— maybe there was a particular way to open it that she hadn't noticed before.

She couldn't help but think there must be more under the latch than just a root cellar. Why would anyone want to lock away a root cellar under steel bars? It didn't make sense, but she also didn't see any other way to open it than the latch.

She tried to work under it to see if the lock would slip backward and satisfy her curiosity. Her hand slipped a couple of times, banging into the floorboard and against the furniture.

"Sheesh!" she said, then sank to the floor onto her bottom. "Nothing's working." She swept her hair backward and leaned against the furniture she'd pushed aside. She was sweating and breathing hard, and the latch remained in the same tight position as it had from the beginning.

Maybe Jake wasn't really after anything, she thought. Or he really knew there was nothing in the basement that was worth anything. Otherwise, he'd have dug it up and made a clean break. The only thing she could think of was that Alan was just trying to get under her skin. *But what do those emails mean?*

Maybe it was time that she had a heart-to-heart with Jake. If he was being shady like Alan suggested, then he'd have to be the one to break her mother's heart. She'd just repaired their relationship, and Nicole would not be the one to hurt her.

She glanced back at the latch and thought about trying again, but even then, she knew she'd just be wasting her time. What she needed was a jackhammer— a simple screwdriver wasn't going to cut it. Besides, the thing had already caused one injury too many. She would not be its second victim. Flustered, she got up. She might as well get back to her original task.

Now that she'd gotten all the distractions out of the way, it was time for her to focus. She made a pot of coffee from the stash she'd started keeping in the store. She sat down again, opened her laptop, and pulled up the file.

Within minutes, she was pouring over one item after another while downing more than her fair share of caffeine.

She didn't realize what time it was until she felt her eyes burning. She rubbed them, yawned, and glanced at the time on the screen— it was ten minutes to one in the morning.

"Wow," she gasped. "I've been here that long?" she spoke to herself, then reached for another cup of coffee and sat on the office sofa.

After a few moments had passed, everything went dark.

Chapter Nineteen

"**N**icole!"

Someone was chasing her and calling her name, but she couldn't make out who it was. She could see the shadows, so she ran barefoot down the street as the white nightgown billowed after her and the loose stones on the ground dug into her feet.

Her heart pounded hard, and it burned. Her throat was dry, and she was running out of breath.

"Nicole!"

All she could see around her was pitch darkness, but she could tell he was gaining on her. Her feet gave way, and she tripped, falling, and getting tangled up in heaps of her dress. *Why is my dress made from this much fabric?*

But she didn't have the time. The shadow was all around her now, and as he reached down to grab her, she let out a piercing scream that broke the night.

"Nicole!"

Her eyes popped open, and she jumped up, her eyes wide, and looked around her for the black shape that had been chasing her. A few blinks later and she realized she was still in her mother's shop. She looked around, then noticed Jake standing over her, so she shrank back.

"Oh, my head," she said, rubbing her temples.

"Bad dream?" he asked and then picked up the coffee pot. "And please tell me you didn't drink all of this."

"What if I did?" she replied, squeezing the space between her eyes to relieve some of the tension.

"Okay," Jake threw his arms up. "My bad. What are you doing here? Did you stay overnight?"

"Uh, I guess so," she said without looking. "Wasn't the plan, but I got caught up. What time is it?" she asked, forcing her eyes open again.

"Eight fifteen?" he returned, but it sounded more like a question.

"What are you doing here this early?" she asked as her suspicions about him began to take root inside her all over again.

"I forgot I hadn't cleaned out the register, plus I like to get here early sometimes to get things ready for opening," he told her, then picked up a rubber stress ball from her desk.

He sat on the edge and began tossing it into the air, but Nicole wouldn't be fooled by his boyish charm again. There was something sinister about him, and she hated how he hid under the disguise of helping her mother. If only she knew what he was, she wouldn't have been so worried about his heart.

"So, when I came in here, you were moaning. What were you dreaming about?" he asked her.

"Nothing," she snapped. "I'm tired."

"But you just woke up," he teased. "You should be running around the shop now with energy, what with all the caffeine in you."

"What I do with my body is my business," she told him, then closed her laptop.

Jake's brows dipped. "I can take a hint," he returned, then got up. "What's gotten into you?" he asked from the doorway. "It's like you're a whole new person."

I'm a whole new person? How about you look in the mirror?

She knew she couldn't say that to him because she didn't have the proof to back up her suspicions. She wished she had more or that the information had come from a less biased source. Until then, she had to keep her emotions in check, just in case Alan was wrong.

The problem was, she was finding it hard to just keep acting as if she didn't hear anything.

"It's all the caffeine," she told him, then wiped her hand down her face again. "It's making me cranky. I'm sorry."

He stared at her for a couple of seconds and crossed his arms, filling up the doorway.

Great! If she was going to act like a witch, she might as well come out and tell him what was bothering her. Except she couldn't, and she didn't want to be around him either. Maybe what she needed was some fresh air.

"I think I'm going to get something to eat or go freshen up or something," she explained, then got up from the desk. Jake remained in his position, observing her. She couldn't get past him without touching him, and she basically tried to weasel her way around him while he stood stoically, his brows knitted, watching her.

"What are you doing?" he asked.

"I'm trying to get out, but you're standing in my way," she told him. "If you would just..."

But it was obvious she was trying to squeeze her way

through without touching him. "I don't understand what's gotten into you," he pressed, still without moving. "One minute, we're having a nice conversation, sharing a kiss, and then you're all but avoiding me. Is something wrong? Did something happen?"

"Nothing happened," she replied sharply, throwing her hands in the air with exasperation. "I just want to get something to eat. Can I do that?"

She dared look up into his dark brown eyes, and the hurt and confusion she saw almost crippled her. She didn't see anything dark and sinister there, and she wondered, for a moment, if she'd let Alan win after all.

But she wasn't going to stand there while she tried to figure it out. She needed to go— to clear her head.

She didn't wait for him to move. She tried to brush past him, but in her clumsiness, her elbow caught a stack of boxes that were piled against the door. The top one tipped and started tumbling, and Nicole jumped back inside to grab it while Jake tried desperately to steady the others.

It was too late. The four of them tumbled to the ground, sending Nicole free-falling into the desk, bumping her hip, and sending a couple of items crashing to the floor.

"Are you okay?" Jake asked when the dust cleared.

There were pens, pencils, erasers, staplers, and sheets of paper scattered on the floor. Jake started to restack the boxes, but a little further from the door. It wasn't until he'd moved the box that Nicole saw the jewelry box on the ground. It was in pieces.

"Oh no," Nicole groaned as she knelt to pick it up. "It's ruined."

"It was already ruined," Jake told her.

She sighed and put it on her desk. She'd clean it up later and fix what she could, but not with him standing in front of her and making her nervous. Besides, he'd think she was a nutjob for being so obsessed with the old, broken jewelry box that she didn't even need for her jewelry. Yeah, she could admit it was a weird fetish, but there was something intriguing about it that she couldn't put her finger on.

Maybe it was enchanted. Someone may have hexed it, and now that she'd found it, she was under its spell. But to do what?

"What's so funny?" Jake asked, and it was then she realized she'd been smiling.

"Nothing," she replied, clearing her throat. "I'm gonna get something to eat. You want anything?"

"No, thanks," he told her.

And that time, she was able to leave the office without incident. She felt a whole lot better when she could think clearly, and the early morning air did wonders for her. She'd had way too much coffee, but it was nothing that a short stack with scrambled eggs, bacon, and wedges couldn't fix. She felt like a whole new person walking out of the diner, but even she had to admit— she was walking right back to her problems.

Jake was nowhere in sight when she returned to the store, and she breathed a sigh of relief. She grabbed her notepad and stationed herself in a section of the store where she wouldn't be very visible.

Her heart raced when she heard his boots clomping on the floor, and she turned at an angle so that she wouldn't meet his eyes. She knew what she was doing was probably silly, but she didn't know what else to do. She wasn't sure of the right move.

Sure, she could just ignore what Alan told her, but what if he was right? It wasn't as if he'd just told her—he'd also shown her the messages. And they sounded just like how Jake would say it. Not because he was a villain meant he was lying, and she had to acknowledge that.

"Hey," Jake said from right behind her, and she jumped, bumping her elbow into a shelf.

"Yeah?" she answered, still focused on her notepad. She was jotting down the descriptions she found on the items.

"I'm heading out to get some stuff. You want anything?" he asked.

"I'm good," she told him. "Thanks." She turned, giving him a weak smile.

He grunted something under his breath, wiped his hand down the corners of his mouth, and walked away. Nicole let out a deep breath when she heard the door chimes signal his exit, and the notepad fell to her side.

"I can't go on like this," she muttered to herself as she turned about. She had to decide. *Confront Jake. Tell her mother. Reject Alan's claims.* Someway somehow, the ball was in her court, and she had to play it.

So far, Jake wasn't coming across as one of *Ocean's Twelve*. He seemed just as confused by her as she was by him, and it was creating a strained relationship between them. Something had to give, but she didn't know what.

It was nothing but silence for the rest of the day until Jake approached her once again. "Are you closing up early?"

"No," she replied promptly. "Why would I close up early?"

"Because today is the gingerbread house competition, and everyone is going. It's like an unofficial Yuletide

Creek half day of work." He grinned. "I thought maybe you'd want to go."

"Oh," Nicole said as she stared at the floor. "I didn't know that. I mean, I know there is a gingerbread house competition, but I didn't realize it was such a big deal."

"Maybe not by itself," Jake explained as he moved closer to her and leaned against the wall. He was in black jeans and a red-and-black shirt that was rolled up at his elbows— his customary look, but one that wasn't growing old for Nicole. He still looked as yummy as he did the first time she saw him, and with his newly shaved face and boyish looks, he was starting to make her feel giddy.

"What do you mean?" she asked him.

"It's not just a gingerbread house competition. It's also a toy drive. Ally's collecting toys for the less fortunate kids at the orphanage and in the hospital or sick at home."

"Ah," Nicole replied, impressed at the initiative. "I didn't know, or I would have gotten some things."

"It's fine. I think I have enough in my duffel bag that covers it for the both of us," he told her with a smile. "That is if you'll go with me."

Nicole wasn't sure why Jake would want to go with her in the first place. She'd been very mean to him all morning, and he knew she was trying to keep her distance. *Why on earth would he invite me anywhere?*

"I don't know. Last time we closed early, there was a break-in," she said in a weak attempt to get out of going with him.

Jake chuckled. "Lightning doesn't strike in the same place twice. Plus, I don't think they'll hit the store one more time this season. It was already abnormal the first time in a place like this."

"Yeah, I guess," Nicole responded and hugged herself, careful to keep her eyes away from his.

"So?" he asked. "Do you want to come? You don't want to miss this one. It's actually a fun one. It's crazy how these women go all out on these competitions."

Nicole felt so awful. If Jake was the scheming, manipulative person Alan had made him out to be, he was doing a heck of a job hiding it. He seemed like too much of a good guy. Genuinely. She felt like an absolute jerk for thinking so poorly of him. She could see that Alan must have had his men crossed— those email letters must have come from someone else.

Or they were not real. She hadn't looked closely. What if they were? What if she'd been avoiding Jake for nothing?

He deserved someone better on his arm at the competition. She would be a hypocrite for even thinking of going with him.

"You know what, Jake? You go and have fun," she suggested, then smiled at him.

He shook his head. "You're not coming?"

"I mean, look at this place. There's still a lot to get done," she replied.

"Suit yourself," he said, walking away. Now, she felt like the evil one. He turned back when he was at the front of the store. "You know what your problem is? You don't know how to get away and have fun. It's all business for you. But you know what they say about all work and no play. I hope you enjoy your evening. I'll go and be with the normal folks," he quipped.

Nicole stood there gaping at him as he left the shop. She was normal. He would have known that if he knew what she was doing.

Chapter Twenty

Nicole stood in the same spot long after Jake was gone, feeling sorry for herself.

He'd hit a sore spot for her. *The nerve of him, talking to me like that.*

She fumed as she walked up and down the aisles in the shop, panting at Jake's outrageous outburst. But the more she walked, the more she realized that it wasn't so outrageous after all. He wasn't wrong. Ever since she'd gotten to town, everything had all been business for her.

She'd had a single-minded focus to help organize the shop and tuck tail and run. She hadn't planned on being there for an entire month, let alone going to parties, caroling, and participating in gingerbread house competitions.

A small part of her had considered the trip to be something of a vacation. A larger part was focused on the shop, and she had executed that with perfection. She hadn't had much of a vacation at all, and all the events she'd attended were forced.

"Oh, god, I'm a wet sock," she moaned as she collapsed into the chair. "Hell of a vacation." She was working as hard as she had back in Seattle. She'd struggled with being on the grind constantly, with nothing to life than the grind and going home to a bath and a glass or bottle of wine. And she'd gotten the chance to ditch that lifestyle, if even for a month, and what did she do with it? She did the only thing she knew how to— work.

She was disgusted with herself as she imagined everyone in town at the gingerbread house competition except for her. Why was she keeping the shop open anyway? Who would drop in to spend any money on antiques?

She could feel the headache coming on, mostly because she wasn't certain what she wanted to do with her life. She hadn't quit her job— it was still waiting for her if or when she got back. It wasn't a job she loved, and she didn't have friends to speak of. Stevie was already away at college, and she only had the holidays to look forward to when she got a break and could come home for a quick visit.

It was a very bleak outlook that was starting to depress Nicole, and she couldn't keep all those negative feelings swirling around in her head and her heart anymore. She and Stevie had always been close, and she respected her opinion and trusted her with her deepest feelings.

She sighed as she picked up her phone and called her daughter. "Hey, honey."

"Mom, where are you?" she asked on the other end.

"I'm at the shop," she replied shamefully.

"What? Why? Everyone's here," Stevie told her. "And you should see the amazing displays. I've never seen gingerbread houses like these anywhere. You don't even want to eat them." She giggled.

Nicole smiled. "I'm sure everything looks great," she

responded, feeling even worse when she heard all the gay laughter in the background and all the jolly Christmas music being played.

"Jake just got here," Stevie said excitedly. "Are you going to lock up and come over before it's done?"

Nicole sighed. "I didn't even know about it until Jake asked me if I was locking up, but I wasn't in the mood for a party," she admitted, then started pacing the small space in the office.

"Uh-oh," Stevie replied knowingly. "That's never good. Hold on," she said. "Let me find a quiet spot."

Nicole waited, trying hard to filter out all the happiness in the background as the noise dimmed, and Stevie spoke again. "Okay, this is better. So, what's going on, Mom? Something bothering you?"

Nicole smiled at how grown up she sounded. Stevie had always been logical and level-headed, capable of making solid decisions on the fly. She wasn't the typical spontaneous artist— she was different.

"It's Jake," Nicole said quickly before she changed her mind.

"What about him?" Stevie wanted to know.

"Did I ever tell you about Alan? That sleazy developer who's been running around town asking everyone to sell their businesses?"

"I heard something of the sort from Grandma. But what does that have to do with Jake?"

Nicole sighed as she prepared to give the long version. "The other day, I went to the library to get some work done, and he confronted me again about selling the store."

"Why can't he take a hint?" Stevie asked, her tone laced with anger. "We're not selling!"

"Exactly. I mean, when I came to town, I was hellbent

on convincing mom to sell, but even if I was going to, I'd never sell it to Alan. I found out the history behind that store, and it should literally be a historic site— not something that a stranger would buy, then bulldoze to install a gas mart or some other stupid venture."

"Exactly," Stevie agreed.

"So, I told him I'd never sell, and he could take his business elsewhere because I don't trust his intentions. You know what he told me?" Nicole said as she felt the rage rising to the surface.

"What?" Stevie asked as if she was perched on the edge of her seat, waiting for the reveal of the real murderer in a horror flick.

"He told me that if I shouldn't trust someone, it should be Jake," Nicole confessed. "Can you believe that?" she asked the question, but she wasn't sure if she wanted Stevie to side with her in being skeptical of Jake or to tell her that she was an idiot for even believing anything Alan had to say.

"Which Jake?" Stevie asked, lowering her voice.

"What do you mean which Jake? Jake! The one and only," Nicole fumed as she picked up her stress ball.

"That can't be right," Stevie told her. "What else did he say? Was that it? Don't trust Jake?"

"No," Nicole continued. "He said that he'd approached Jake first about selling, and Jake had told him not to come to us about it— that he would help him to get it, but he wanted a part of the commission."

"No way! That's bull!" Stevie blurted out.

"Right?" Nicole asked excitedly. "That's exactly what I thought. No way would Jake do that to mom. But then, he showed me some email messages between the two of them, where they were arguing over who gets what out of the commission. He wants me to believe that Jake was upset when he found out we know about Alan because he was afraid Alan was going to cut him out of the commission."

"Okay, first of all, we're not taking any advice or evidence from a snake," Stevie ordered matter-of-factly. "Secondly, that's not the Jake that I met. I know I'm only twenty-two, and I haven't met a lot of men to compare, but Jake is a pretty decent guy. And thirdly, have you told him any of this?"

Nicole felt her face warm at the question. "No," she replied. "I didn't know what to say."

"Uh, how about, 'Hey, Jake. I heard some shady stuff about you. What's the deal?'" Stevie quipped.

"That may sound easy to you, but it's been hell for me," Nicole admitted. "I didn't want to say anything to him about it until I had some more facts. And I didn't want to say it to mom because I didn't want to hurt her feelings."

"So, you just kept it to yourself, and now it's eating you alive instead?" Stevie pointed out.

"Not my intentions," Nicole groaned, then sat on the edge of the desk. "I was just working my way around to believing the email message must have been fake, that no way would Jake undercut Mom like that. I preferred keeping it to myself than saying it, just in case it was false, and then it'd be weird between us."

Stevie sighed. "I get the feeling you're way past weird by now if you've been keeping secrets for days. I say you should just man up and ask him about it. That's not an accusation. Just ask him. See what he says. What's the worst that can happen?"

Nicole exhaled. "You're right."

She recalled how her same actions had cost her years of a relationship with her mother. If she'd been open from the start and had let her mother in on how she felt about the divorce and the accident, they could have been spared years of pain. She was already in the beginning stages of repeating her old mistake, and she didn't want it to cost her.

"When did you get so smart?" Nicole asked Stevie.

"I had a good teacher," Stevie replied. "Grandma."

"Ha, very funny!" Nicole laughed. "I'm so proud of you, though. You've grown into a remarkable young woman."

"Thanks, Mom. Now would you please lock up the shop, come over, find Jake, and you two have a talk? And just so you know, I'm also rooting for you two."

Nicole blushed. "Thanks, sweetie. I'll see about locking up."

"Okay, later, Mom. Love you."

"Love you too, baby," Nicole told her, then bit her lower lip as she hung up the phone.

Ever since Rudy left, most times, Nicole couldn't tell who the mother was and who the child was when it came to her and Stevie. She had so much wisdom in her tiny frame that often blew Nicole away. Her response to her just then had been precise and cut right to the thick of it. She hadn't hesitated on what she thought the right thing to do would be.

She suddenly remembered the mess she'd made in the office earlier after her little debacle with Jake. It wasn't as bad as she thought, and she gathered the stationery items and then picked up the jewelry box. It wasn't that bad, but one side of the box was now crooked, and as she lifted it, she heard a faint rattling sound.

"Shoot. It's even more broken," Nicole said out loud and shook the thing. Yep. There was definitely a rattle that wasn't there before, but it wasn't something she could readily see. She turned it around and pressed on the inside seams, but she finally guessed that it might be an old part from the mechanics that had fallen off and was stuck inside.

She stared at it, then shook her head. "So, the one piece of thing I like in this glorious junkyard seems determined to get broken?" she asked as she laughed at herself for refusing human company, and there she was, in the shop, talking to an old, broken jewelry box.

Everyone had been right about her. But she'd show them. Besides, she had a man she needed to find in order to make things right once again.

So, with her heart drumming a beat, sweat beads pooling over her face and causing her palms to get clammy, despite the winter cold, she threw her coat over her and stepped out into the frost.

It was time for her to get to the bottom of the Jake mystery once and for all. And for once, she hoped she'd been wrong.

Chapter Twenty-One

She could feel her nerves pricking all the way to the Christmas House. And Jake wasn't wrong— it seemed all Yuletide Creek was there.

The streets leading up to the house were filled with parked cars, so much so that she could barely get a spot, and when she finally did, it was on the parallel street. She pulled up behind a string of cars and began her trek to the house itself.

Her heart did a nosedive when she saw Jake's truck. She was afraid she'd have a heart attack before she even got a chance to speak to him. She didn't know she could feel that love-struck again because she was certain that was what it was.

Her eyes roamed in search of that clean-shaven, handsome face she'd grown fond of, but maybe it was dumb luck— she seemed to have found every other one but his.

"Nicole, right?" someone asked from her right as she walked, and she glanced over to see that it was Mayor Luke.

"Hi, and yes." She smiled at the man.

"Good to see you out and about enjoying all of what Yuletide Creek has to offer." He grinned.

"You too, Mayor," she replied, leaning closer. "I'm a little surprised to see you at all of them, considering your reputation." Heck, if she was going, to be honest, she might as well lay it all out there.

He chuckled. "You mean how much of a grinch I am?" he asked jovially.

Nicole laughed too. "Yes, that. I didn't expect you to take it to...to..."

"To heart?" he asked. "Well, sticks and stones, right?" He smirked. "I figured I'd earned it too. But I'm the mayor. I have to be at these events. I just didn't think I should be spending on things that seemed unimportant when the town has so many bigger problems."

"I hear you," Nicole told him. "That's very smart, though."

"But what can I say?" he asked and spread his arms. "Sometimes, there are people who get to you and make you do things you wouldn't normally do."

"Yeah." Nicole laughed, thinking about her own situation. "I know exactly what you mean."

He patted her arm. "Good seeing you, Nicole. I hope you enjoy the festivities."

"Thanks. You too, Mayor," she replied.

"Oh, please. Call me Luke." He winked, then waved as he backed away.

She felt a whole lot better after that. The people in Yuletide Creek must have been given an extra dose of happiness and Christmas spirit. There were glowing cheeks everywhere, and she received warm smiles from everyone who seemed overly eager to point her where she needed to go.

She hadn't seen her mother or Stevie yet, but she wanted to see Jake first. The thing was, there were a sea of people, and she didn't want to go asking anyone for him. She knew how small towns worked— perhaps the very next day, she would hear all sorts of gossip about her supposed relationship with Jake. And small-town folk weren't shy with their gossiping either— some would be daring enough to come right up to her with their questions.

She'd rather wait until she knew what she wanted to do before she let anyone else in on what she was feeling.

Nicole began to feel exasperated when, after a while, she couldn't find Jake. Her heart leaped when she finally did, but he was busy playing with some children in the back. She was sure she'd walked past that spot several times, but now that she'd found him, she had to wait with her heart in her throat and her mind going a mile a minute.

"Hey," he said, jogging over to her when he spotted her. "I thought you weren't gonna come."

"Yeah, I wasn't," she told him, kicking at a mound of earth. "Someone changed my mind."

"Someone?" he asked suggestively and wagged his brows.

She laughed. "Yes, my daughter."

His face fell. "And here I was thinking it was me."

"It was her idea, but you're the reason why I'm here," she told him as she looked around. "This is a pretty decent turnout."

"Yep," he agreed. "It usually is. They're gonna have some caroling inside in a couple of minutes, and I believe Santa Claus is here too."

"Wow. I don't think I'm high up on Santa's nice list this year," Nicole joked.

"Yes, you've been pretty naughty...to me." He mock pouted.

She couldn't help but laugh at his silliness, but she had an agenda, and if she didn't say it to him soon, she might grow cold feet and never do it at all.

"I know," she told him. "Do you have a minute?"

"Sounds serious," he returned as his smile completely disappeared.

"Depends," she said and took his hand. "Let's find somewhere we can talk."

They walked to a small track close to the road where they wouldn't be interrupted. He stood in front of her with his legs apart, his arms crossed over his chest and his gaze locked onto her face. "Okay, what's going on?"

Now that Jake stood in front of her, Nicole's mind went blank. Her lips were parched, and her throat was dry and scratchy. Her nerves were getting the best of her.

"Well?" Jake asked, egging her on. "You wanted to talk, and here I am."

"Okay," she said breathlessly as if she'd just run a mile. "I don't want you to take this the wrong way, but I just had to ask, and I know I should have come to you before instead of letting my mind run away with me. I should have given you the benefit of the doubt and..."

"Nicole," Jake said, stopping her. "Just tell me, would you? You're making me really nervous."

"All right," she said, inhaling deeply. "You remember Alan?"

"I do," he replied, scratching his head.

"Well, remember how he wanted to buy the shop, and

we all told him no?" Jake shook his head in acknowledgment. "One day, he cornered me at the library."

"You mean that day when you chickened out and didn't come into the shop after we kissed?" he asked her pointedly.

Nicole blushed. "I'm not agreeing to or denying that, but yes, that same day,'" she replied, and Jake chuckled. She thought she'd been fooling him, but as it turned out, she'd only been fooling herself. He'd read her like a book and had been doing so all along. No wonder he wasn't mad at her— he must have known how confused she'd been all this time.

"Go on," he coaxed, waving his arm before crossing them again.

"Well, I was at the library, and he came at me again, asking if I'd reconsidered convincing my mother to sell. He even knew why I was in town, which I found very creepy. Anyway, I told him we weren't interested and how much I didn't trust him. He told me that the person I shouldn't trust is right under my nose, and I don't even know it."

Nicole paused there for emphasis and to gauge Jake's reaction to her statement. He stared at her like a deer in headlights, completely baffled by what she'd said. "Who?"

"You!" Nicole blurted out. "He told me I should be wary of you."

"Me?" Jake asked, tapping his chest. "Why? What did I do?"

Nicole hadn't finished telling Jake the whole truth just yet, and already she felt like an idiot for even thinking he might have been mixed up with Alan. "He said you and he were in bed together over the shop and that you'd promised to help him get it for a huge commission."

Jake stared at her still, and then he started to laugh. "Hold on, let me get this straight. Alan and I had a deal to split the commission on the sale of the shop. And you believed him?"

"I didn't know what to believe," Nicole said softly, avoiding his gaze.

"No, you believed him," he said, walking a few feet away, rubbing his head in the process. "Well, at least now I know it wasn't my kiss that was so bad," he shot when he turned back to her. "But I knew something was going on with you. I just didn't know what it was, and I certainly wouldn't have guessed that. But tell me something, Nicole," he came to stand right in front of her, forcing her eyes to his, "why would you believe that man?"

"Because he showed me email messages between the two of you?"

Jake's eyes popped. "What? He has email messages? Between me and him?"

"Yes," she replied. "I saw them. Why do you think I was confused?"

"What did they say?" he asked.

"Just a chain of messages back and forth with you and him arguing over commission, who's to get what, and you negotiating what you think you should get and that he shouldn't approach us. So, when I told him I didn't believe him because you were angry when you heard that he was trying to sell the shop, he said you were just angry that you were being cut from the commission."

"Wow," Jake replied, wiping his hand down his face. "That's a pretty elaborate lie. Fake email messages? The manipulation. I mean, I get why you'd be skeptical because you didn't know me, but from what I know about commission...wait, how much did he say I was to gain?"

"Hundreds of thousands," Nicole told him, feeling even sillier the more she talked.

Jake erupted into laughter. "I don't know. The shop wouldn't be worth that amount of money, and he'd only be getting a percentage of the selling price, which would give me a percentage of that. How on earth did you believe I could get hundreds of thousands out of that?"

"I don't know. I wasn't thinking," Nicole admitted. "And I have to say, telling you now and hearing it out loud, it does sound rather stupid."

"If I wanted to get the shop sold, I'd have just tried to convince Mrs. Hayes myself. Why would I want to cut him in on it at all? I don't think he thought this through."

"And neither did I," Nicole said as she blushed again. "I feel so stupid."

"You've been keeping this inside for a whole week?" Jake asked, surprised.

She nodded in the affirmative. "As I said, I didn't think it through, and he seemed convincing. But it was Alan, so I wasn't sold all the way despite the evidence he presented. And then there was you. I couldn't reconcile the Jake I met and that my mother constantly vouches for while Alan made you out to be something entirely different. That was what was eating at me."

"I see," he replied. "There shouldn't have been any doubt in your mind. Clearly, Alan is a weasel. Why would I be emailing him? And when would it have happened? Did you look at that?"

"I didn't look that closely," she confessed. "I guess he knew I wouldn't."

"I see," Jake returned as a mischievous grin appeared.

"What?" Nicole asked.

"You know, your mother did warn me about you." He smirked.

"Is that so?" she asked, then crossed her arms over her chest.

"Yep. She told me how much you were set in your ways and always think you're right. How does it feel to be wrong for the first time?"

She cocked her head to the side. "Well, she also told me how you're a delicate, soft flower and how I should be careful I don't hurt your big, kind heart."

Jake's voice boomed with laughter. "Delicate flower? Come on," he quipped, pulling her to him and crushing her against his chest. "Does that feel like a delicate flower?"

"Nope." She laughed. "Feels more like the rough side of a cliff."

Jake continued laughing, and when he stopped, he was staring into her eyes. "Are you really planning on leaving town after the holidays?"

"I don't know," she told him as she tried to ignore the way his heart was beating in unison with hers and how his musky scent was making her drunk with desire. "Is there a reason I should stay?"

"I was hoping you'd found one," he replied huskily, his voice deeper than it had been before.

"Maybe I have," she returned. "I just wasn't sure what to do. I was thinking about that before I came here. I just don't like my life back in Seattle like I used to. It was bad before I left, but after being here, what can I say? Yuletide Creek is growing on me."

"Is it just Yuletide Creek, or something specific about this small town?"

She laughed because she knew what he wanted to say,

but like a cat, she liked playing with her meal. "No, not just the town. The people here are nice too. I mean, there's Mayor Luke. He isn't so bad. Not a bad-looking guy either."

She felt Jake's arms slip from around her as his face scrunched up, and she doubled over in laughter.

"Mayor Luke? That's a reason to stay? And not me?"

"Yeah, maybe you too." She giggled.

"I'm going back to the kids. They're more fun. They actually like me," he teased, walking off.

Nicole giggled at his silliness and ran to catch up with him. "Okay, fine. You're my main reason for wanting to stay so much."

He threw his arm around her as they walked back to join the rest of the community. "I thought so," he replied, kissing the top of her head.

She was glad she'd been wrong about him, but one thing still weighed on her mind. What was Alan up to? And why would he weave such an elaborate lie about Jake?

Chapter Twenty-Two

Everything was different after that.

Nicole was super anxious to go back to the store after that, and Jake found every excuse he could find to work where she was.

Trisha noticed and cornered Nicole when she was leaving the office one morning. "So, I see things are heating up nicely," she teased.

"Mom." Nicole blushed. "We're going slow. Don't worry. I won't break his little heart," she said, then pinched her mother's cheek in passing.

"Oh, don't forget the guys are coming today to install the new window," Trisha said excitedly.

"Ah, right," Nicole replied, stopping in her tracks. "How on earth did you find someone willing to come out here at this time?"

"Luck, I guess," Trisha beamed. "The owner was pretty much packing up, but when he heard Yuletide Creek, he changed his mind. Said he's come to town a couple of times over the years, and he'd hate for me not to have my window display."

"That's so nice of him," Nicole said. "It will liven things up for sure. It's been so weird being behind this wooden barrier."

"I know, right? Now I can start my displays all over again."

Nicole rolled her eyes. "Yeah. I live for those."

Trisha chuckled and nudged her shoulder as she returned to the register. Nicole returned to the floor to add some prices to the items she hadn't already tagged.

The men came to install the glass, and surprisingly, it didn't take as long as Nicole thought. They were finished in just under two hours.

"It's a beautiful sight." Trisha grinned, then thanked them profusely as they loaded up their supplies and left. "Now," she started to say, rubbing her hands excitedly. "Time for one more display before Christmas. Oh, I'm so excited," she squealed, then skipped off. Nicole had no doubt she'd get carried away with the display.

Jake returned from his chore just in time to see her with an armful of ornaments and lights snaking behind her.

"Whoa!" he said as he quickly rested the paper bag on the counter. "I'll get those."

"Oh, thank you, dear," Trisha replied. "But there's more back there."

"I got it," Jake told her.

"What about your wrist? Is it all better?" Trisha asked with wide eyes, and Nicole snickered.

Jake knew exactly why— it was that delicate flower thing again. "It was a minor thing," he said, holding up his bandage-free hand. "All better."

"Oh," she responded. "Well, there's a box back there. And another in that corner behind the register.

"Hey, I thought this was my job," he said as he walked away.

"I have special plans for this one," Trisha beamed.

"Okay, then," Jake returned. "Just let me know if you need any help."

"Maybe with the lights," she told him. "I'll handle the rest."

Nicole shook her head. She could see that her mom was going to have a field day with that display. She was pulling out the whole North Pole to put in the display area. Nicole was supposed to be pricing items, but she was fascinated with how excited her mom was. And also annoyed— her mother kept removing items she was yet to tag, which meant she'd have to go back over the shelves again when she removed the display items.

"Mom!" an infuriated Nicole cried, then stomped her foot. "Don't you think that's enough? You're going to crowd the display area."

Trisha chuckled. "Sorry, but I need these."

"Need is a strong word," Nicole replied with a sigh and resumed her tagging, but she was constantly on the watch for a busybody Trisha.

Nicole had completely forgotten about her after a while until she saw the display coming to life. It was coming around to her time for a break, and she walked over to her mother to see the progress she'd made.

"Wow," she exclaimed, but it was more sarcasm than awe. It looked like a giant smorgasbord of random items from the store. Nicole leaned over and picked up a little Annie doll. "I don't get it. Why do you even need this?"

Trisha yanked it from her and replaced it on the soft bedding she'd made for it. "Never you mind that."

"So, you didn't get a chance to have any displays for

the last week or so, and now you're just going to mash all the ideas together? That's the theme for today?"

Jake chuckled from behind her. "I think it's interesting."

"Of course, you'd think so," Nicole said, throwing up her arms.

"Thank you, son," Trisha beamed. "That's why I'm going to leave the shop to you and not her," Trisha teased.

"Ha!" Nicole blurted out. "My loss, I guess." She rolled her eyes. "But come on, Jake. How is this even about Christmas? There's a nutcracker over there standing beside what looks like Little Bo-Peep. And what's this?" she asked, picking up a little toy soldier. "Mom, no one is even going to see this."

"Someone will." She grinned. "You'll see."

"I thought this would be more Christmassy," Nicole said with great disappointment.

"Well, look who's gotten into the Christmas spirit," Jake joked.

"It's not that," Nicole replied and blushed. "But if you're going to have a display for Christmas, then have Santa, the elves, the nutcracker, and the nativity scene like everybody else."

"But we're not like everybody else, are we?" Trisha retorted with her hands on her hips. "This is an antique store, and for me, this is more than just a light show. It's advertisement. Someone will see something in the display that they'll like, and they'll want to come in and have a look around."

"She makes a good point," Jake said from his position against the wall.

"I don't care what you say. I don't think anyone is going to spot that little toy soldier in the back. Or this golden egg," she said, picking up the bedazzled oval piece. "This actually looks nice."

"See? Something already caught your eye. Thank you for proving my point." Trisha smirked.

Nicole growled and narrowed her eyes at her mother. "I can't believe I walked right into that."

"Aren't you getting tired of being wrong?" Jake asked, adding insult to injury.

"I see this is a team effort to make Nicole look bad," Nicole pouted, crossing her arms.

"Nope," Trisha replied, then added some candy canes closer to the front. "I was just over here doing my business, and you came over to make fun of me, so that's what you get."

Nicole narrowed her eyes again and pointed from a chuckling Jake to a smug-looking Trisha. "You two drive me crazy," she cried out, throwing her arms in the arms.

"But think about it," Trisha told her. "All of this that's here," she said with a sweeping gesture of her hands, "it's just a little reminder that there are hidden treasures all around us."

Nicole shook her head. "That's exactly what hoarders say," she returned, nodding profusely.

"We'll see who's right after Christmas," Trisha beamed as she stood. "There. All done."

"Good job, Mrs. Hayes," Jake complimented, then patted her shoulder. "Some people just don't know how to appreciate art. They must not have that in Seattle."

Nicole couldn't help laughing, and Trisha joined in. "Very funny, Jake. But speaking of hidden treasures, I need to show you something."

"Well, you two run along. I have some errands to take

care of," Trisha said, reaching for her purse that was under the counter.

"Mom, please don't bring another rocking horse in here," Nicole begged.

Trisha winked at her. "I can make no such promises."

"Ugh, you see what I have to put up with?" she asked Jake when Trisha breezed through the door.

He laughed. "She's a sweet old lady."

"I know," Nicole agreed, rubbing the back of her neck. She'd been bending and stretching into weird places all morning, and her body had begun to protest.

"Let me," Jake said, coming up behind her. "I know how this store can give you kinks where kinks shouldn't be."

Nicole smiled as he started rubbing her shoulders, and all she could think of were his hands on her and her kinks already forgotten. She grinned when she remembered his kiss, and her body began to tingle. She moved slightly, forcing his hand to fall away. She couldn't be held responsible for what might happen if Jake kept his hands on her.

"So, you remember that old jewelry box I'd found?" she asked as they got to the office.

"And you talk about your mother being a hoarder? Nicole, that thing's useless. Just throw it out," he told her as she picked it up.

"I think there's more to it than meets the eye," she replied, holding it out to him.

He took it and looked it over. "Looks busted up and not worth a dime."

"Maybe," she took it back from him. Then she shook it. "Do you remember hearing that rattling before?"

"I don't know." He shrugged. "I wasn't paying close attention. Or obsessed."

"It wasn't," she said, glaring at him.

"But didn't it fall at one point? I mean, it's old. Probably just broke off a part inside," he suggested.

She sighed. "That's what I was wondering. I didn't hear the rattling until after it fell off the desk," she said, turning it over in her hands.

Trisha returned shortly after and hurried into the office. "What are you two doing in here?" she asked, looking around frantically.

"What are you looking for?" Nicole asked.

"My pocketbook," she replied. "I thought it was in my purse."

Nicole glanced at the desk. "There it is."

"Oh, good. I thought I'd lost it," she said, then spotted the jewelry box. "Hey, what are you doing with that?"

"That's what I've been asking," Jake replied. "I told her to throw it out. It's junk. But she's fascinated," he said, making spirit fingers as he said 'fascinated.'

Trisha laughed. "And that's not just junk. It's old junk."

Nicole knitted her brows together. "What does that mean?"

"It means, that's junk I inherited. It came with the place. I just didn't think I should throw it out."

"Of course not," Nicole retorted. "You throw nothing out."

But what her mother said intrigued her even more. She started pushing and pressing sections of the box, working her way around it.

Jake crossed his arms and looked at her suspiciously. "What are you doing?"

"Looking for a hidden compartment," she told him as she held up the box again and shook it. "The noise is coming from the lid."

"Why would there be a hidden compartment, Nancy Drew?" he asked mockingly and took the box from her.

"I don't know. That's what I want to find out."

Her curiosity rubbed off on Jake, and soon he was doing the same thing— pressing the inlay that would magically reveal an opening.

After a couple of minutes, they realized their effort was futile. "I'd just say something broke off when it fell. It's old. That's not much of a mystery. But," he said, holding it up to the light as if it was transparent or hollow.

"What?" Nicole asked excitedly.

"We could see what the rattling is if we smash it open," he offered softly and turned it over in his hands. "But it would be nice if we could actually see in it without smashing it open because once it's smashed, that's it, and I wouldn't want you to lose sleep over it," he mocked, grinning at her.

But what he said gave her an idea. "You know what? You may be onto something."

"About you losing sleep?" he asked, chuckling.

"No, about seeing inside without breaking it further," she returned as her eyes lit up. "Come on." She grabbed his hand, adrenaline coursing through her as she picked up her purse and headed for the door.

"Where are we going?" he asked as she hauled him outside.

"You'll see," she said as they got into the car, and she drove off, the wheels of the car squealing as she peeled out down Main Street.

Chapter Twenty-Three

"The clinic?" Jake asked when the car pulled up in the small parking lot at the back of the building.

"Yep," Nicole replied excitedly and slid out of the car.

"Why? Nothing's wrong with my wrist," Jake said, hopping out of his side. "What are we doing here?"

"You'll see," Nicole told him. "Come on."

Jake was very apprehensive as he walked after her into the clinic. Like before, there were several people in the waiting room— all seats were occupied, and some people were pacing the floor and flipping through magazines while they waited.

"This place gets so busy during the holidays," Jake mumbled.

"Such a shame," Nicole said as she walked up to the receptionist who recognized her.

"Hi, how are you?" she asked.

"I'm good, thanks," Nicole told her.

"How can I help you today? I hope nothing too serious," she said with concern, looking around Nicole. "We're drowning today...practically have to turn people away who can wait."

"Too bad, but no, we're not injured or anything," Nicole told her. "But does that mean that Dr. Weaver is tied up?"

She glanced down at a chart before she looked up again. "Uh, yeah, he's in with a client right now."

"Is there any way I can get a quick word with him? I promise I won't take up too much of his time," Nicole beseeched.

"I don't know," she replied, then picked up the phone. "Let me see if he can reach him."

"Thank you," Nicole said, breathing a sigh of relief.

The receptionist held the phone close to her lips and shifted to an angle where Nicole could neither see her lips moving nor hear what she was whispering. She waited with bated breath as the woman turned back to her with a smile on her face.

"You're in luck. He has about ten minutes to spare. He'll be out shortly."

"Thank you so much," Nicole returned as she stepped away, and Jake practically attached himself to her side and whispered in her ear.

"I still don't know why we're here and how it's going to help with the box," he questioned.

Nicole was just about to answer him when she spotted Dr. Weaver heading in her direction. "Nicole," he greeted, extending his hand to her.

"Hello, Doc." She smiled, fixed her purse on her shoulder, and shook his hand in greeting.

"Come with me," he told them, walking off. "Sally said you wanted to see me about something. I hope it's to hand in your resume." He grinned, stealing a glance over his shoulder at her, his pale gray eyes twinkling.

She blushed. "Uh, not yet. I'm still working up to it."

"I hope you do soon. I could use all the hands I can get," he said as they got to his office and stepped inside.

It was the typical doctor's office with a large desk by the window with a black, worn leather chair accompanying it. The desk itself was neatly arranged with files, a picture of two beautiful women, and then of another with a bunch of people sitting by a fire at Christmas, all decked out in red and white onesies.

"Is that your family?" she asked out of sheer curiosity.

"Uh, yes," he replied as he sat. "Please, have a seat."

"They're beautiful," she told him. "Those your daughters?"

"Yes," he said, picking up the frame. "Samantha and Robin— my prized possessions." He beamed as his eyes grew nostalgic. "But don't tell them I called them that. They tell me I make them sound like things." He chuckled, setting the picture down again. "But they're all grown now. Have their own families in Seattle."

"Seattle? That's where I'm from. Maybe I've bumped into them before." Nicole smiled.

"Perhaps," he said wistfully.

"It's great how much you adore them. I have a daughter of my own from a previous marriage," Nicole said, then cleared her throat.

"Oh, divorced?"

"Yes," she replied, fiddling with her fingers.

"I lost my Emily about six years ago. Breast cancer," he said sadly, then glanced back at the group photo. "That was the last photo we took together before she got sick."

"I'm so sorry to hear that," Nicole told him. "I don't

usually know what to say to things like that— words never seem to offer much comfort."

He chuckled. "I know what you mean. But you can do like everyone else and bring me a tuna casserole because nothing shows support like a tuna casserole."

Jake laughed. "Ain't that the truth?"

"Okay," the doc asked, leaning forward in his chair. "What did you need from me?"

"Oh, I almost forgot," Nicole said, glancing at her purse. "I just needed a favor."

"Name it." He smiled at her. She couldn't tell where she'd ever seen eyes that kind. He had to be a doctor, and he must be a really good one too. He made her feel safe, and she could tell his patients felt the same way.

She took out the broken jewelry box and showed it to him. "There's something inside it, and I want to know what it is, but we can't get it open, so I was wondering if you'd be so kind as to loan me your X-ray machine."

She felt Jake move next to her as if he'd shifted so he could look at her. "Right," he said as realization hit him. "You what?" the doctor asked, narrowing his eyes at her.

"I know it's a pretty unconventional thing to ask, but I was an X-ray technician. Still am, and I know my way around the machine. I'll be quick," she explained hastily.

"You're right. That is an unconventional request. And you say something is inside it?" he asked, holding out his hand for the box.

Nicole placed it into his large palm, and he lifted it up to the light as if Jake had done before, then he shook it. "I see what you mean. And there's no opening? Sounds like a broken spring."

"That's what I thought." Jake nodded.

"I just want to be sure. I've grown a certain...fascination for it," she said and blushed.

Dr. Weaver gave her the jewelry box and sank into his chair with his fingers steepled under his chin. "Tell you what? I'll allow this on one condition."

"Uh-oh," Nicole replied, cocking her head to the side.

"I'll let you use my machine if you will actively show an interest in working here. Give me your resume," he told her.

"Oh," she said. She hadn't given more thought to working at the clinic, but with her renewed interest in remaining in Yuletide Creek, having a job she'd enjoy would be like the cherry on top of her Yuletide Creek sundae. "I can do that."

"We have a deal then," he said, then sprang up. "I mean, I would have let you use it and all, anyway. It's Christmas, right?"

"Doc, did you play me?" Nicole asked, and his laughter echoed in the halls.

"Maybe." He winked. "I still got game."

Both she and Jake laughed as he led them to the end of the hall and into a small room. "There it is. You know what to do, but I have to get back to my patients. It was nice talking to you, Nicole."

He was walking out when she got an idea. "Hey, Dr. Weaver," she called.

He stopped abruptly in his stride and wheeled around. "Yeah?"

"You don't have family in town, right?"

"Nope. Not a one." He smiled. "Why?"

"I don't know," she responded. "Christmas is the worst time to be alone, and I know that from experience."

"I planned on being here," he replied. "I have a lot of patients who need care."

"That's even worse. How about you come over and have Christmas dinner with us?" she asked, already seeing how he could be a good fit for her mother. She'd practically pushed her into Jake's arms. It was about time she returned the favor. Plus, Dr. Weaver was too nice of a man to spend Christmas alone.

The smile he gave her lit up his entire face. "Thank you. I'd like that."

"Okay. I'll leave the details with your secretary. See you then," she replied as he closed the door behind him.

"That was really nice of you," Jake said as they walked up to the machine. "Genius, by the way," he told her.

"It was the first thing that came to mind when you mentioned seeing what was inside without smashing it."

"I can see that," he said as Nicole powered up the machine and prepped it. "But I don't get why you had to be mysterious about it."

"It's one of my charms." She grinned. "Okay, let's see what this mystery box is hiding," she said and set the box on the bed.

She pressed the button, and the machine whirred to life, slowly gliding on the beam overhead, its laser passing over the metal box and creating an image neither of them could decipher.

"Maybe it only does people," Jake suggested when it seemed it didn't work.

"It's not that," Nicole explained, then reset the machine. "I've scanned more than people before. Maybe if I change the angle," she muttered, mostly to herself, as she turned the box onto its side.

The machine whirred again, and they watched as the light passed over the box. Nicole took up the print from the machine again, thinking about how convenient it was, rather than all the way down the hall like it was at her previous job.

"What's that?" Jake asked as he squinted at the printout.

Nicole turned the page from side to side, both of their necks craning to see what the image was. "Maybe it'll clear up in a few minutes," she said, already feeling as if it was a waste of her time.

"It looks like a key," Jake said after a couple of seconds. "See that long part there and the jagged points on that end?"

"I think you're right," Nicole agreed as her breathing started becoming shallower. "Let me shake it and do it again."

She did, and the next printout was as clear as day. "Oh my god, Jake," she exclaimed and covered her mouth. "It's a key. So, it was a mystery, after all."

"Yeah," Jake replied less than enthusiastically. "You just found an old key to go along with an old jewelry box. Yay, us!" he said with mock excitement.

Nicole snickered. "I thought I was supposed to be the sarcastic one." Then she turned her attention to the key again. "Why would a key be locked away so precisely in a jewelry box? It doesn't seem like something someone wanted other people getting their hands on."

"Maybe it's all the gold that's buried under the shop. The original owners were pirates. Or maybe, when the Spanish conquistador came, he left a treasure trove."

Nicole cocked her head to the side. "Really? You're not at all curious what the key is for?"

"Nope," he responded honestly.

"Well, now that we know it's a key, let's get it open."

"Oh, now you don't care about all the intricate details that make it up?" he teased.

"Jake, just open it," she demanded.

"All right. If you insist," he said, placing it on the floor. With one stomp of his right foot, the jewelry box gave up the ghost. And the key.

He reached down and picked it up. "Here you go. You now officially have the key to my heart."

Nicole giggled and blushed. "That easy, huh?"

"Yep," he replied with a smile.

"But seriously," she returned, staring at it. "What could it be for?"

And suddenly, their eyes lit up, and she grabbed Jake's arm.

"The hatch," they said simultaneously, right before they blew out of the clinic like a tornado.

Chapter Twenty-Four

"I don't remember even seeing an opening of that size," Jake protested on their way back to the shop. "Maybe it's not for the hatch."

"One way to find out," Nicole replied with great enthusiasm. "I knew there was something special about that box," she beamed.

"Hold your horses," Jake cautioned her. "If it's a key for the lock, we still don't even know what's down there. For all we know, it's just mold and dead animals."

"I love your optimism," Nicole quipped as she glanced over at him.

He chuckled. "I try."

She could barely park the car properly when she got back to the shop, but her excitement over the hatch was quickly tempered when she saw a gloomy Trisha sitting by the counter, her palms holding up her jaw.

"Mom, what's wrong?" Nicole asked, the key in her purse temporarily forgotten. Her mouth moved up and down as if she wanted to say something, but no words came out, which only frightened Nicole more. "Mom!" she said again.

"I'm fine," she responded, obviously upset.

"You don't look fine. What's wrong?"

"That darn developer guy. I knew he would try to do something like this," she grumbled.

"Do something like what?" Jake asked protectively, moving forward. "What did he do."

"You know how he's been all over town asking people to sell? Well, we just found out that he doesn't even want to own the shops. All he wants to do is bulldoze them and put up some apartment complex."

"What?" Nicole asked. She had her suspicions, but for them to be confirmed just widened the sinking feeling she'd had in her gut into a full-blown chasm of doom. "Who told you this?"

"He did," she replied, sliding a piece of paper over to Nicole. "It's all in there."

Nicole grabbed the paper, and Jake stood behind her, looking over her shoulder as they read what it said. "They can't force you out," Nicole replied angrily. "This is your shop, and the choice is still yours."

Trisha rocked, and her lips tightened into a slit on her face. "I don't want to sell, but you know how these guys are. And none of us have the original deeds for the shops. Most of that information was lost in the great blaze." She sighed. "They will find a way. They always find a way, and then we will have to work for them. That's how cities are formed."

"It doesn't have to happen here," Nicole returned furiously, slapping the paper down onto the counter. "No one has to sell their businesses because some greedy developer has his eyes set on it!"

"Hey, Mrs. Hayes," Jake said, taking her hand. "Don't worry about it. We'll get to the bottom of it."

Her eyes changed when she looked back at Nicole and Jake again. "You two seemed pretty excited when you burst in earlier. What was it that had you so happy-go-lucky?"

"Oh, this," Nicole replied as her earlier excitement returned. She reached into her purse and took out the key.

Trisha looked unimpressed. "Is that a key?"

"Yes!" Nicole said, with wide eyes, like the single, rusting key should mean something to her mother.

"Nicole believes it can open the hatch at the back of the store," Jake explained.

"So?" Trisha asked. "What do you think is down there?"

"I don't know." Nicole shrugged. "But there's only one way to find out."

She hurried off with the two in tow and didn't even wait for Jake to move the furniture again.

"It may need oil or something to grease the joints," Jake observed. "That thing's old."

"Maybe," Nicole replied as she knelt on the floor and looked at the keyhole. "Looks like the same," she said, trying to slip it inside. It wouldn't go all the way. "Come on!" she commanded, trying to jiggle it.

"I'll get the oil," Jake told her. "But stop jiggling it. You'll probably break it off in there."

"You're right," Nicole relented, pulling the key out. "I'm so anxious to find out what's in there to warrant a secret key hidden in a jewelry box."

"Yes, it's weird," Trisha said as Jake returned with the oil.

He poured some over the keyhole, then against the hinges. "Try it now," he told her.

That time the key slipped further into the slot, but it wouldn't turn. "Let me try." Jake knelt next to her.

She scooted over so he'd be over the latch, and after a few attempts, it turned, and the latch popped.

Nicole gasped, covering her mouth. "It's open!" she said ecstatically. "Man, I'm so glad I didn't throw out that jewelry box."

"Again, opening the hatch isn't the discovery," Jake reminded her. "Let's just see what's in it first."

"Probably a couple of dead rats and raccoons," Trisha said as she leaned over to look.

"I don't care what either of you say," she said as she stood back for Jake to lift the door open. "No one hides something that isn't valuable. And by the way, if I'm right, I'm not sharing anything with either of you."

Jake laughed and then started coughing when the door opened, letting out a gust of musty air that was suffocating. "Yep," Jake said as he rested the door against the wall. "You can keep what's down there."

Nicole chuckled and shook her head, but she took caution as she peered into the hole. "There's a couple of steps. I need light," she said as she hurried back to the office, where she procured a small flashlight.

"Excuse me," she told both reluctant spies who were still just standing around looking at the hole in the floor.

"You're not seriously going down there, are you?" Trisha asked worriedly.

"How else am I going to know what's down there?" Nicole asked as she shed her coat and prepared to enter the opening. "But you're right," she said as she coughed too. "It is musty down there."

"Maybe you should wear a mask," Trisha suggested.

"Great idea, Mom," she replied, stopping in her tracks. "Can you grab one for me?"

"I'll get it," Jake told her. "No way you're going down there alone."

He returned with two masks a short while later and handed one to her. They both slipped them over their face and ventured into the small, cramped space.

"Ooh!" Nicole gave out when her foot touched something squishy. "What is that?"

She shone the light at her feet and realized she was walking on paper.

The space was big enough for them to stand without hitting their heads against the ceiling but not so big they could fit more than what she saw.

"No treasure here," Jake said as the light hit several stacks of boxes and files on a rickety table. "Just paper."

"But what kind of paper?" Nicole asked as she walked over to a box and opened it. She picked up the first file she found. "Here, hold this for me, please," she instructed Jake and held out the flashlight.

He took it from her and shone it onto the file she was holding. She squinted as her eyes adjusted to the poor lighting, and as she read, she realized what it was. "This can't be right," she said, picking up another file.

"What is it?" Jake asked, not being able to make sense of what she was reading.

"These are old records," she explained. "Yuletide Creek records. Dating back to the eighteen hundreds."

"Quit playing," Jake said as he took the file from her and pored over it. "Damn!" he exclaimed when he saw the date on a parcel of land belonging to the Millers.

Nicole began to search frantically through some

other boxes and was ecstatic when she found the old blueprint for city hall. "Jake," she said, gripping the front of his shirt as excitement seized her again. "I think this used to be the basement of the original city hall. Look!"

"Original?" he asked as he looked at it. "There was another one."

"I remember the librarian was telling me how there was a huge fire in the eighteen hundreds that wiped out this whole section of the town. All the town records were lost. This is huge!"

"I'd say," he replied, scratching his head. "This is crazy."

"Are you two doing okay down there?" Trisha asked from the opening.

"Yes, Mom. But you won't believe what we found," Nicole replied. "Help me to bring one of these boxes up. I'm going over to the library. The librarian will be able to vet all of this. And won't Mayor Luke be happy to have all of this information intact?"

"Guess you were right," Jake said as he picked up a box. "This is a treasure, but it belongs to the town."

"I wasn't expecting gold," Nicole said as she walked off after Jake. "Heck, I don't know what I was expecting, but it wasn't that."

"What's this?" Trisha asked when Jake pushed the box through the opening before he snaked his way out. He turned to give Nicole a hand before he turned to Trisha again.

"Town records," she told her mother, even as she dusted cobwebs and dust from her clothes.

"You missed some," Jake said, lifting even more cobwebs from her hair.

She laughed when she saw he had the same. "You too." She pointed, so he started rubbing his head as well.

"What do you mean town records?" Trisha asked. "Wouldn't those be at city hall?"

"Mom, it looks like this was the old city hall," Nicole said excitedly. "There's all kinds of town records dating back over a hundred years."

"Everyone thought those were lost in the fire," Trisha exclaimed, looking at a few sheets of paper in the box. She gasped and covered her mouth.

"Mom, do you know what this means?" Nicole asked excitedly. "No one will have to fold to Alan and his bigshot friends. I can bet the deeds are in there somewhere."

"That's right," Jake grinned. "This is really great news for everyone."

"We should tell people," Trisha said right away.

"Precisely what I was thinking," Nicole replied. "I wanted to go to the library to have the information vetted, but it seems pretty legit to me."

"Me too," Jake agreed.

"Well, what are you waiting for?" Trisha asked as she hurried off. "Let's go!"

It didn't take long for the town to come alive with the news. The librarian had a field day with the information Nicole showed to her, and in a matter of hours, the whole town, including Mayor Luke, congregated in and out of the antique store.

Mayor Luke and Jake finished emptying out the cellar, revealing stacks of boxes and dusty files.

"This is just amazing," Luke said, hugging both Trisha and Nicole. "Wow. You know what that means, right?" he asked with a wide grin.

"No," Trisha replied, shaking her head, then looked at Nicole in confusion. "What?"

"It's just a matter of formality and all, but you are officially standing inside a historic landmark. This is the only piece that's left from the original city hall and all the buildings that were on this street. This place will have to be preserved."

There was a loud applause and a ring of laughter as everyone cheered.

"This is the only thing I need for Christmas." Owen grinned.

"Me too," the baker returned. "Now I don't need to sell my shop. Mayor, can I help with sorting out the papers? I want to make sure my shop documents are inside."

Mayor Luke laughed. "Don't worry, everyone. We got everything out. We'll hand over anything that you all will need. In the meantime, y'all can go about your business as usual. I've got it covered."

There was a series of happy mumblings as the crowd dispersed, and Nicole and company shook Luke's hand before Jake helped him to get the boxes onto his truck.

"Isn't this the best Christmas ever?" Trisha asked as she threw her arms around a beaming Nicole.

"You bet," she said as she squeezed her mother tightly. "It's the best one I've ever had!"

Chapter Twenty-Five

"**W**ake up, everybody! It's Christmas!"

Nicole's eyes fluttered open, and she blinked rapidly. *Is that Stevie?*

"Mom! Grandma! Wake up!" she yelled from the hallway.

"Stevie?" Nicole groaned, rising onto her elbows, her eyes still reluctant to open fully. She turned her head and saw that the sun had barely broken over the horizon.

"Mom, it's Christmas!" she declared again as she came into the room that time.

"I know, but I'm still tired," Nicole groaned. "How old are you again?"

Stevie giggled as she tried to pull her mother out of bed. "Everyone's a kid at Christmas!"

"Not me," Nicole protested as she tried to reposition herself.

"Nope," Stevie stated as she tugged on her mother's shoulder. "No sleeping in today. We have lots to do," she told her mother.

"Okay fine," Nicole relented, "before you give me a

dislocated shoulder." Stevie laughed and finally stopped. Nicole sat on the edge of the bed, rubbing the remainder of the sleep from her eyes. "What are you wearing?" Nicole asked when she saw the red, green, and white onesie Stevie had on.

"What? This is my Christmas outfit." She grinned. "I have one for you too."

"No thanks," Nicole told her. She got up, stretched, yawned, and fell on her face on the bed again.

"Ugh!" Stevie growled, pulling at her legs that time.

"Okay." Nicole laughed as she kicked free of Stevie's hold. "I'm up."

"Good," Stevie beamed. "Only rule for today is no regular clothes. You have to wear Christmas colors."

"You mean the only *other* rule, the first being no one is allowed to sleep past seven on Christmas morning!" she yelled and tossed a cushion at a fleeing Stevie, who then doubled back to stick her tongue out at her mother.

Nicole inhaled deeply and laughed to herself after Stevie had gone. Maybe the last time she'd had a Christmas resembling anything she was experiencing was way back when she was in Yuletide Creek as a kid. Despite her parents' differences, they'd made Christmas fun for her. Even though her daughter was twenty-two, she felt as if she still owed her the same courtesy.

"Fine," she said to herself as she stood in front of the closet. "What do I have that looks like Christmas?" she asked as she started to slide the clothes aside. She saw a red-and-white sweater she didn't remember bringing with her. She took it down. *Nope— that's brand new.*

She smiled when she realized that must have been Stevie's early Christmas present. "Very funny, Stevie," she said as she took out the sweater. It was just her size and taste as well— if nothing else, she knew her mother well. She quickly washed up and donned the sweater and a pair of black leggings she had. *This will have to do.*

Of course, her mom was wearing the same sweater when Nicole got downstairs, and Stevie greeted her with a pair of green socks with elves and candy canes printed all over it.

"Of course, we get matching socks too." Nicole giggled. "Thanks, honey."

"You're welcome," she beamed, slipping a hat onto her head.

"Mom, what are you making?" Nicole asked. "Need some help."

"I'm almost done, but I have..."

"Sticky buns, Christmas coffee with whipped cream and all, and French toast casserole," Stevie answered excitedly as her stomach growled. "Grandma, please tell me it's ready."

Trisha and Nicole laughed at how distraught Stevie looked. "They're in the oven as we speak. It shouldn't be more than another couple of minutes."

"Good," Stevie replied, clutching her stomach. "I'm dying."

"Must be from all of that screaming, yelling, and pulling people from their beds earlier," Nicole said.

Trisha chuckled. "Spirited, isn't she?"

"That she is," Nicole answered as she remembered how she used to do the same thing to her parents when she was younger. Much younger.

"I think we can get the coffee now," Trisha attested, then walked off to get the Christmas mugs. Of course.

"Yes!" Stevie hissed.

Trisha poured the coffee into the cups and added her

spices of cinnamon, cardamom, and sugar, mixing lightly as she went. A dollop of whipped cream covered the sweet fragrance before she topped it with green and red sprinkles.

"I don't know," Nicole said as she stared at her cup. "I'm afraid to mess this up."

Stevie giggled. "I get it." And then she licked a third of the cream from the cup.

"Well, that didn't last long." Nicole snickered as the three women sat by the kitchen island, donned in their Christmas outfits, drinking coffee.

"I didn't think we'd ever do this," Trisha told them. "I'm so happy we're all here. Together."

"Me too." Nicole smiled. "I wouldn't have it any other way. Makes me feel awful for all the Christmases I wasted."

"Yeah," Stevie said as she poured into her cup. "I have a couple of friends who didn't even leave campus to go home because they would have nothing like this. I'm so happy and grateful that I do." She rested her head against her mother's shoulders.

"I've missed this," Nicole admitted.

"We can do it again next year. Bigger and better!" Stevie suggested excitedly.

"How about we just take it one day at a time," Nicole advised, much to Trisha's amusement.

"I'm game, baby girl," Trisha replied. "Maybe next year, she'll be the one pulling us out of bed." She chuckled.

"I highly doubt that," Nicole insisted and finally sipped her coffee. "Oh my god, this is heaven!" she declared as she threw her head back and closed her eyes. "You have got to tell me what you put in this."

Trisha laughed. "It's just cinnamon and sugar," she responded. "Nothing special."

But it was, and in no time, they were all done with the coffee. Trisha got the casserole and the buns, and they dug in, getting a sticky mess all over the counter.

"I'm so full," Nicole groaned afterward.

Trisha packed up the leftovers and placed them in the fridge right before she took the marinated turkey out and popped it into the oven.

She told Nicole, "It's almost ten, and we have lots to do by three when our guests start to arrive."

A smile spread across Nicole's face when she thought about seeing Jake later that evening. She rolled herself off the counter, and in no time, she was busily making gravy, stuffing, carving out cranberry slices, and making the batter for the cornbread while Trisha focused on the salads, turkey, and green beans, and Stevie made her all-famous shrimp pasta.

The dinner table was already dressed in silver and crystal, and Trisha's fancy gold embroidered napkins when both Jake and Dr. Weaver arrived promptly at three.

They were both carrying gift bags, which Stevie happily took and deposited under the tree with the others. "Merry Christmas," she greeted the men.

"Merry Christmas," they replied simultaneously as Nicole took their coats.

Nicole was surprised to see them wearing red sweaters and black pants, and she narrowed her eyes. "Did Stevie put you both up to this?" she asked.

Dr. Weaver chuckled. "Yeah, we heard there was a dress code."

Nicole shook her head. "Welcome to the party." She grinned, pointing at her socks.

Jake said. "I see you're fully oriented now."

"Quite so." Nicole giggled. "Come in, make yourself at home. Dinner is ready, by the way. We figured we'd just get right to it, and then we can, you know, hang out afterward when we can't move."

Jake laughed loudly. "That much food, huh?"

"You have no idea," Nicole said softly. "I think she's expecting the whole town."

"I heard that," Trisha teased as she brought out the turkey and placed it in the middle of the table.

"I was thinking of a little icebreaker before we ate," Dr. Weaver began as his eyes trailed after the turkey and he started to salivate, "but scratch that," he said and walked after Trisha as if she was the pied piper, and he was the mouse.

Jake and Nicole snickered as they followed him into the dining room.

"Oh, I see you're all ready," Trisha said when she turned and saw four pairs of hungry eyes bearing down on her turkey. "In that case, take your seats wherever you feel most comfortable."

Nicole helped her to bring out the rest of the food items, which couldn't fit on the dining table— Trisha had to pull up another table to rest some of the other items.

"You weren't kidding," Jake replied as he rubbed his hands together.

"It's a meal fit for a king," Dr. Weaver beamed. "These smell wonderful, Mrs. Hayes."

"Thank you, Dr. Weaver." Trisha blushed, and then she and Stevie shared a mischievous look. They were both thinking the same thing, and then they hung their heads and giggled. They'd play cupid after dinner.

"You know, before we dig in, I just wanted to say that this Christmas is especially wonderful for me. I have my two precious girls here with me after so long," Trisha said as her eyes became glossy.

"Oh, Mom," Nicole replied softly, already feeling overwhelmed by all the emotions.

"It's true. I'm really thankful for new beginnings, for mine, and for yours," Trisha finished her sentence. "That's all I wanted to say.

"Well, you sort of just opened up the floor," Nicole joined in, "so I'll add that I'm glad I stayed for Christmas, even though I didn't really come for it. I stayed away far too long, and I'm just happy to be home."

"Me too," Stevie added. "I didn't really know much about Grandma except for the short visits over the years. This is the first time I've ever really hung out with her, and Grandma, you're awesome!" Stevie grinned.

"Aw," Trisha said, brushing away her tears. "I can't believe your all are making an old woman cry.

"Nothing wrong with that," Dr. Weaver chimed in. "As for me, I'm grateful for new friends and also a brand-new start."

"I guess that leaves me," Jake said. "I'm grateful for a lot of things. Mrs. Hayes taking me in like a stray cat and treating me like a son," he said amid the giggles. "I'm grateful for good company and even better food and a fresh start." He stared right at a blushing Nicole.

"Okay, I think we can make a fresh start on this food now, right, Grandma?" Stevie asked impatiently.

Trisha laughed. "After grace."

"Fine," Stevie groaned.

They all held hands as Trisha said grace, and then they all dug in as if they hadn't eaten in days. There was a lot of laughter and chatting as they teased each other, and the soft sounds of Christmas carols playing in the background made for the perfect Hallmark movie.

After dinner, they all lounged lazily in the living room, feeling like sloths.

"I don't think I can take another bite," Stevie moaned.

"Me neither," Nicole replied.

"I heard about that discovery you made at the shop," Dr. Weaver said to Nicole. "That was pretty awesome. It was an awful thing to have lost all of the town's history, and now to find it again?"

"I know, right?" Nicole beamed. "Now everyone has a rightful claim on their properties. No more bullying from Alan. Where is he, by the way?"

"I heard he tucked tail and ran out of town as soon as the discovery was made," Jake said. "All's well that ends well."

"I guess," Nicole said.

They spent the rest of the evening chatting and laughing until it was time for Dr. Weaver to leave. Jake helped with clearing the dishes, and soon after, they all engaged in a game of cribbage.

"This should be a new tradition," Stevie suggested.

"What?" Nicole asked as she set the board down on the coffee table.

"The day we had today," she said as her eyes lit up. "We can have the same breakfast, the same activities, dinner with mostly the same things, the outfits, and then we all play cribbage and Christmas movies to end the day."

"That doesn't sound like a bad idea at all." Trisha smiled. "I'd like that."

"Me too," Nicole agreed.

"Does that mean I'm invited?" Jake asked brazenly.

Stevie raised her brows. "Duh!"

And they all erupted into laughter. "Okay, okay," he beamed after. "Let's play."

They engaged in about two hours of gameplay, with Jake winning most of the games, much to their dismay. Before they settled into eggnog and cookies and a Christmas movie, Trisha went upstairs, and Stevie wandered off with her phone, leaving just Jake and Nicole in the living room.

"So, a new tradition, huh?" he asked.

"Yep." She smirked.

"Does that mean you're going to come back every Christmas, or you're just going to stay?" he asked as he played with her hair.

She grinned as her insides warmed to him being that close to her and to the thought of him being a permanent part of her future. "Depends. Do you want me to stay?" she teased.

"Do you even have to ask?" he asked her.

"Maybe," she joked, then bit her lower lip.

"I want you to stay," he confessed just before he leaned forward and lightly kissed her lips. "I want you to stay."

"Then I'll stay," she murmured as she reached in and kissed him back, firmer, more definitively. When their eyes opened, they were staring into each other's eyes.

"I have something for you," he said, pulling back and taking something from his pocket.

"What's this?" she asked as she lit up.

He handed her a rectangular black box, and her heart beat heavily as she opened it with trembling fingers. It was a golden locket on a matching chain. "Oh, Jake, this is beautiful."

"I know how much you love shiny things and secret compartments. I figured this would fit the bill." He smiled, stroking her cheek.

She reached up and held his hand in place. "Thank you," she beamed as she clasped the piece of jewelry.

He looked deeply into her eyes. "You're welcome. Merry Christmas," he said before he kissed her once more.

Coming Next in the Yuletide Creek Series

You can pre order A Christmas Wish

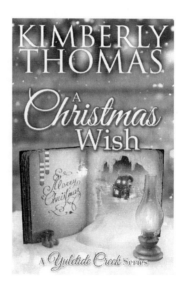

Other Books by Kimberly

An Oak Harbor Series

The Archer Inn

A Yuletide Creek Series

Connect with Kimberly Thomas

Facebook
Newsletter
BookBub
Amazon

Made in United States
North Haven, CT
21 October 2023

43031235R00122